Fitness After 50 Workout

Fitness After 50 Workout

By Elaine LaLanne
with Richard Benyo

THE STEPHEN GREENE PRESS
PELHAM BOOKS

THE STEPHEN GREENE PRESS/PELHAM BOOKS

Published by the Penguin Group
Viking Penguin, a division of Penguin Books USA Inc., 40 West 23rd Street,
  New York, New York 10010, U.S.A.
Penguin Books Ltd., 27 Wrights Lane, London W8 5TZ, England
Penguin Books Australia Ltd, Ringwood, Victoria, Australia
Penguin Books Canada Ltd, 2801 John Street, Markham, Ontario, Canada L3R 1B4
Penguin Books (N.Z.) Ltd, 182–190 Wairau Road, Auckland 10, New Zealand

Penguin Books Ltd, Registered Offices: Harmondsworth, Middlesex, England

First published in 1989 by The Stephen Greene Press/Pelham Books
Published simultaneously in Canada
Distributed by Viking Penguin, a division of Penguin Books USA Inc.

10 9 8 7 6 5 4 3 2 1

Photography by Jim Stimpson

Library of Congress Cataloging-in-Publication Data
LaLanne, Elaine
    Fitness after fifty workout / by Elaine LaLanne, with Richard
Benyo.
        p.   cm.
    ISBN 0-8289-0669-6
    1. Aged—Health and hygiene. 2. Middle aged—Health and hygiene.
3. Exercise for the aged. 4. Cookery (Natural foods) 5. Physical
fitness for the aged—Forms. I. Benyo, Richard. II. Title.
III. Title: Fitness after 50 workout.
RA777.6.L36 1989   89-32590
613'.0434—dc20   CIP

Printed in the United States of America
Set in Palatino

Contents

THE PIONEER IN BODY PART DEVELOPMENT—Jack LaLanne still works out daily on resistance machines that he invented 50 years ago, and that set the standard for today's fitness studio industry. His machines are very much body specific in their application to building, flattening, and toning various muscle groups.

Foreword

EVERY PART CONTRIBUTES TO THE WHOLE

When I opened my first health spa in 1936, people were not into fitness. They were not aware of the benefits of physical activity—not educated to the benefits of systematic exercise and working out. My concepts of weight-training at that time were so advanced that they were not only incomprehensible to the average person, but doctors, coaches, and other authorities failed to understand them. The "experts" of the day did not understand what could be accomplished with systematic exercise and scientific nutrition.

As a result of pushing my views, I was considered a charlatan, a real quack. But today, in the midst of the physical fitness boom, I find myself preaching the same messages I preached in 1936. Even the equipment I invented 50 years ago is still used today to provide resistance for muscle development. The hindsight of 50 years has changed me from a quack to an authority.

It seems that everyone with whom you come into contact these days is into fitness of one kind or another. They're into vitamins, proper diet, swimming, walking, jogging, or aerobic dancing. Almost everyone is doing something to increase their physical fitness and health. This makes me tremendously happy. My life's work has been to get every man, woman, and child into physical fitness. Never has the number of people into fitness been larger than it is today.

During the more than 30 years when I broadcast my TV show, I received hundreds of thousands of letters. It has always been gratifying to me to learn of the positive results people have gotten from watching me on TV. A certain pattern became apparent in reading those letters. It was interesting to note the number of people who were concerned with certain problem zones: the waist, the hips, thighs, double chin, round shoulders, fatty pads on outer thighs, fat knees, turkey-neck, flabbyseatitis, and on and on. It was to take care of specific body parts that I designed my program not only to include something for all parts of the body, but to do the exercising non-stop. Doing exercising non-stop for at least 12-15 minutes makes it aerobic.

Maybe you are already doing something aerobically, such as bicycling, swimming, walking, jogging, or aerobic dancing. These exercise routines are great for your cardiovascular conditioning. But now you can add another dimension to your cardiovascular conditioning: body specific exercises: workouts for the hips, thighs, back of the arms, waist, posture, etc. All these areas need specific work, and that's what Elaine has done in this book.

In this book, you will not only be concentrating on your cardiovascular conditioning, but you will also get down to the real nitty-gritty: your problem zones.

When people get into physical fitness, they not only want to feel and look good and be healthy, but they want to have a real streamlined body so they can be proud of it.

I'm proud of Elaine for writing this book. She is going to help multitudes of people to really reach their goals and if you follow the program in this book, I believe you are going to get results that you never dreamed possible.

So let's get your act together and let's strive for physical perfection. It's yours for the doing!

—Jack LaLanne

Introduction

We live in an age of miracles. It is an age exploding with knowledge. People who keep score on such things tell us that mankind's knowledge doubles every 10 years. What that means is that within the last 10 years, there has been as much knowledge uncovered, discovered, and formulated as there had been in the previous 10,000.

In our own lifetimes, we have seen polio vaccine invented, men walk on the moon, and computers go from the size of boxcars to the size of a portable typewriter.

There is so much knowledge in so many fields that people have had to specialize. We've seen the family doctor (the general practitioner) practically vanish. In his place are doctors specializing in internal medicine, cardiology, and surgery, etc.

There are no longer "shade-tree mechanics" when it comes to automobiles. Automobiles have become much too complex. There are now mechanics who specialize in one automobile make or another.

Beauticians now specialize in hair, face, or nails, and advertising agencies target their advertising to special groups according to age, income, ethnic tastes, education, and a battery of other criteria.

It seems logical, then, that in this world of increasing specialization, when we are dealing with our own health and fitness, we should specialize to some degree. We should consider customizing our bodies to our liking by making use of certain laws of nature that can be made to work on our behalf.

How many people actually think about customizing their bodies with a very specialized program? I know that I didn't.

When I met Jack LaLanne I was 27 years of age. I considered myself old. I looked at myself and I thought that as we age, our bodies just grow out and around just as my mother's and my grandmother's had. It was just a law of nature, a natural evolution associated with aging. I did not, at that time, realize that you could actually change the proportions of your body through exercise and proper nutrition.

If you've read my previous two books, *Fitness After 50* and *Dynastride!*, you'll recall that I was one of the original junk food junkies. I was working at KGO-TV in San Francisco as a Girl Friday. (Today my job designation would be co-host.)

My diet consisted of donuts, Danish rolls, candy bars for lunch, canned foods, soft drinks, and practically no fresh fruits or vegetables, and I smoked cigarettes. Eight years had passed since I had exercised consistently while swimming in the Minneapolis Aqua Follies. My life had been essentially sedentary for those eight years.

Jack aired his show on KGO-TV from 9:00-9:30 every morning. When I would arrive at the station with my chocolate donuts, he would often say, "You know the only thing good about the donut is the hole in the middle because it has no calories."

I thought that was rather funny, but kept right on eating them anyway, until one day his enthusiasm, sincerity, and dedication got to me. I went home and took off all my clothes and looked in the mirror and saw that the sands of time were shifting. My chest was sinking into my waistline and my legs had that doughy, wash-board look (That they today refer to as cellulite.) and I thought to myself: "Can anything really be done about this figure?"

I soon joined a class that Jack had started at the station for some people who wanted to exercise. I went every day and lo and behold, I saw a change in about a week. Within a month I saw a big change. And within three months I saw a complete change. It was like a miracle!

Jack explained to me that every cell in your body changes every 90 days, except for the central nervous system. So my new eating habits and exercise program had really paid off. The reasoning behind it seemed so logical, so uncomplicated, I found that I, too, wanted to share it with the world. I noted that Jack's television show concentrated on all areas of the body. The letters poured in from viewers about the results they were getting from watching and participating in the show.

One of the reasons that people were getting results was that Jack always gave an exercise for every part of the body and even exercises to do while watching the commercials. Viewers were getting about 27 minutes of non-stop exercise. That is the premise of the word "aerobics"—doing non-stop exercise so that you get the heart rate up and keep it up. Jack believed in a complete workout with complete movements and he wanted each person to develop a near-perfect body.

As the fitness movement progressed, people were dancing, jumping, riding bikes, jogging, and doing anything they could to give themselves an aerobic workout. The fitness craze was in full swing! It became evident, however, that the fitness enthusiasts were getting a great aerobic workout, but what was happening to those special problem zones of the body that were not getting attention? Areas such as the back of the arms, the chest, neck, face, sides of the waist— the list goes on…

We are frequently asked about the various programs in aerobics, weight-lifting, dance, etc. Our only comment is: "You wouldn't just wear black shoes or red shoes all the time." Everything you do physically is important as long as you don't overdo it and that you have regular check-ups. If you belong to an aerobic class, for instance, try to incorporate specific exercises for specific parts of the body into your program. When you do the same thing all the time, the muscles get used to it and they don't respond as readily. The muscles need to be challenged and that is why it is important to change your program about every two to three weeks. And remember, "Variety is the spice of life."

Since the human body is such a complex machine, we must appreciate it as the end product of many integrated parts. Each part—each muscle and ligament and joint—has a function on which many other parts depend. For instance, weakened abdominal muscles and protruding waistlines are one of the primary causes of a weak lower back.

Many of us have lived our whole lives with body parts that are troublesome, embarrassing,

and personally disappointing. These areas include heavy legs, flesh drooping under the upper arms, and weak abdominal muscles that cause bad posture. Sometimes the task of changing those troublesome parts of our body seems overwhelming. But these troublesome zones can be improved by concentrating specifically on them through positive action: scientific exercise and proper nutrition.

"But," you're saying, "I'm over 50 years of age! *I* can't change my body this late in life! Can I?"

The simple answer is that, "Yes, you can change and contour various parts of your body— one part at a time." It doesn't matter how *old* you are. What matters is how *young* you want to feel and look. I'm sure you've seen 25-year-olds who have bodies that look over 50, and 70-year-olds who are as spry as though they were 25 years old.

Imagine, if you will, a fine old house or a classic car that has provided years of faithful service. All those years and all those miles *do* pile up, certainly. The house needs structural repairs and the window frames need to be repainted and weather-stripped and the roof has a few small leaks. And the classic car? The upholstery is torn and the top is tattered and the horn doesn't work and the tires are bald.

To look at either the house or the classic car would be depressing.

But seen through the eyes of a good carpenter or a good auto mechanic, the house and the car represent challenges. The carpenter and the mechanic are not going to attempt to restore the house or the car in one day. They'll examine the situation carefully and proceed one step at a time.

The carpenter may feel that the most pronounced problem on the house is the roof. After all, it's no use sanding the hardwood floors inside if the roof allows water to leak onto them and ruin them all over again. So, he tackles the roof first. With the roof done, the interior isn't going to deteriorate any further from outside forces. He's made a start. People passing by and seeing the new roof are going to remark: "Why, look at that old place! Somebody's beginning to fix it up!"

The same applies to the car. The mechanic sands down the body panels and repairs rust spots and someone who sees the car knows right away that it's being restored.

And that's what this book is about: Changing yourself one body part at a time, all the while building toward a more perfect you.

Begin working on that pot belly or that sagging flesh under the upper arms or that double chin and pretty soon people are going to notice that there's work going on to restore that classic body.

But more importantly than other people noticing, *you're* going to notice that there are improvements being made, both internally as well as externally, mentally as well as physically.

What special qualities are needed to be a person who is able to restore him- or herself? Not many, really. Desire, pride and discipline, and the will power to stick to your commitment of exercise.

So let's take your rather classic body and restore it. I can't promise that it will look exactly as it did at 19 years of age. But what I can guarantee is that if you work with me to restore it, part by part, you'll feel better, you'll look better, and you'll be healthier overall because once you've made the improvements, maintenance will be relatively easy. In fact, it will be fun—so much fun that you'll look forward to each new day as you never have before.

—Elaine LaLanne
Morro Bay, Calif.
November 1989

PART ONE

How The Aging Process Can
Be Controlled

Chapter 1

How Time Erodes The Human Body

I can't think of any other subject that makes its way onto the best seller lists more consistently than books on diet and exercise, even though some are more than a little faddish and unsound. This obsession with weight and diet is an area of real concern because, according to recent studies, most Americans are "overfat."

Notice that I didn't use the term "overweight." "Overfat" designates a condition of having too much body fat relative to lean body mass, or as I call it, good muscle tone.

To better understand this concept, let's take a bodybuilder, for example. When the bodybuilder steps onto a bathroom scale and takes that weight along with his or her height and applies those numbers to the widely accepted height/weight charts, the bodybuilder is going to appear to be overweight. In actuality, however, this is not true. Because the bodybuilder is on a scientific program of exercise and nutrition, working all parts of the body, the "excess" pounds are invested in muscle mass, while there is very little body fat involved. Muscle, you see, weighs more than fat.

Merely looking at the numbers would indicate that I am overweight. I'm 5 foot 3³/₄ inches. My measurements are 36-25-36. And I fluctuate between 116 and 120 pounds. If I happen to go up over 120 pounds, I take it off right away. Most people who take a quick look at me think I weigh between 105 and 110 pounds, but my extra 10

pounds comes from muscle mass. So you can see that we might very well call the term "overweight" a misnomer. Therefore, for the sake of accuracy, let's use the term "overfat" even though the term "overweight" seems to have more of a familiar ring to it.

Jack has written many times on the subject of "Your waistline is your lifeline." He has stated that the scales do not tell the truth. For instance, you might weigh the same as you did 20 years go, but your waistline is 4 or 5 inches wider, indicating that you are overfat. What you've done over those 20 years is lose 30 pounds of youthful muscle and gained 30 pounds of fat.

We can be overfat in specific parts of the body and not in others. It is the distribution of this fat with which we have to be concerned, since it tends to gravitate to and exaggerate our body's problem zones. For instance, how many women have problems with overfat buttocks and thighs? How many men find the fat gravitating toward the middle, contributing to pot bellies and love handles? You see, fat is like a river: it will flow to that part of the body that has the least resistance.

Please note at this point that my "body specific program" is based on your problem zones and on the fact that you are already engaged in a regular program of exercise and nutrition as outlined in either *Fitness After 50* or *Dynastride!* At various junctures in this book, I will address what steps should be taken if you feel compelled to start work on a body part but do not have a fitness base established. Just as you would not put a roof on a house before building the foundation, it's important to be engaged in that regular fitness program in order to take the next step. In fact, you may have already begun to see the body fat vanish, to be replaced by muscle mass.

Let's take a look at how the average person puts on excess fat. Actually, putting on excess fat is quite easy!

Americans have two major factors which make them overfat.

1. Exceeding the Feed Limit. (Yes, this is another famous LaLannism.) Americans have access to more quantity and varieties of food than any other nation on earth. Food here is plentiful. In fact, the U.S. is the greatest food producer in the world. Many people exceed the feed limit by over-eating one meal a day. Some exceed the limit by not realizing how many times a day they pick and snack out of the refrigerator.

Other causes are: compulsive nibbling, eating improper food combinations, learning bad eating habits from parents, overconsumption of dairy products, etc. Remember these other LaLannisms: "He that stuffeth, puffeth." "What you put in your mouth today is walking and talking tomorrow."

2. Lack of Exercise. Many Americans lead lives and have jobs that do not require them to move. Automation in the home and years in professions that involve a lot of sitting have undermined the amount of calories a person burns each day.

Excess body fat comes from taking in more calories than you burn up.

As we age, this fact is exaggerated because the metabolism furnace inside each of us that burns calories in order for us to function begins to slow down; nature puts dampers on the human furnace. So, even if we cut down our food intake as we age, we can *still* gain body fat because we burn food slower.

Consider this example of how easy it is to put on weight:

If you eat *one* LifeSaver per day beyond the caloric requirements of your body, in a year you will be carrying around one pound of excess fat. If you are 50 years old, that means you're carrying around one excess pound per year of life, or 50 excess pounds. See how easy it is? In most cases it isn't something that happens overnight. It is a process that creeps up on you a little at a time.

What problems crop up with being "overfat"?

a. Heart disease. Much of the excess fat Americans gain comes to them through foods high in cholesterol. Cholesterol causes plaque to form inside the arteries, eventually closing them off, which in turn robs the heart of blood. Additionally, the "overfat" person is less likely to exercise, and exercise strengthens the heart muscle; lack of exercise allows the heart muscle to atrophy—to the point that when the least bit of strain is placed upon it, it can collapse under the workload.

b. High blood pressure. Excess fat directly contributes to high blood pressure, and high blood pressure is a major factor involved in heart disease. It has been medically shown that when a person begins to lose fat, blood pressure usually drops.

c. Diabetes. Excess fat is a major factor in a person's proclivity toward diabetes, and diabetes can cause a multitude of problems, including blindness, chronically poor circulation, potential amputation, etc.

d. Chronic lethargy. The more excess fat a person is carrying around, the more tired and lethargic that person is going to be. Consider the extra work involved in pulling yourself out of a chair if you weigh 175 pounds as opposed to if you weigh 135 pounds. Further complicate the process of pulling yourself out of the chair by the fact that if you have excess fat, you likely do not have well-developed muscles that the slimmer person may have, and the process becomes doubly difficult. It becomes much easier just to remain sitting in the chair, doesn't it?

e. Poor self-image. Most people who work hard to get rid of excess fat do so because they don't like the way they look. Self-image can be a good motivator. Nobody *really* wants to look like a beached whale. People *want* to look and feel healthy and fit, but in most cases they either don't know how to go about reaching a healthy and fit state, or they are unable to get together the necessary motivation. The irony with the low self-image caused by being overly fat is that it often causes great emotional stress, which in turn often causes overeating, which, in turn, causes more and more fat to accumulate. It becomes a vicious circle, and all the time, the self-image continues to drop.

The basic formula involved in losing body fat is very simple:

Calories In - Calories Out = Weight Loss

(As long as the number under Calories Out is larger than the number under Calories In.)

The ideal way to lose body fat is to exercise regularly because exercising burns calories, not just while you are exercising, but for hours afterwards. By exercising regularly, you significantly increase your Calories Out number. Many people find that as a result of a regular exercise program, they don't have to play around with their Calories In number at all. The increased burning of calories just naturally uses more calories than are taken in, and there is a subsequent loss of fat, with a consistent toning of the muscles.

It should be noted that in instances where a person begins exercising regularly to lose fat, there may be no change in weight. In fact, there might even be an increase in total body weight. This is due to the fact that the person's exercising is building muscle tissue while burning fat; muscle weighs more than fat. So it is misleading to rely on the bathroom scale. You should, instead, rely on a full-length mirror. By taking a critical look at yourself in the full-length mirror, you'll *know* whether or not you are in good shape. And notice how your clothes fit.

Do not, however, continue to be obsessed with body *weight*. It is a very unreliable yardstick. As you get farther and farther into your fitness program, expect to see a redistribution of body weight. Once you have progressed to the level of my Total Body Program for Life in Part III of this book, you're likely to be well on your way to the ideal you.

A cautionary note: Before embarking on any exercise program, have your family doctor do a thorough physical on you. The check-up can pinpoint any areas of concern that might dictate how fast you begin exercising, the type of exercising of which you are capable, and how often each week you can exercise safely. Then, schedule another physical every year in order to keep track of your progress. Remember, too, that if you took 50 years to get out of shape, don't push yourself to get back in shape overnight. Patience and good pacing wins the long race. One thing a person over 50 has usually learned is how to establish a good pace. Pace yourself well and your body will respond with surprising results.

WHY MUSCLES LOSE TONE

When I was a little girl, we spent many summer vacations at my grandparents' house in Roland, a small town in Iowa. Each year I couldn't wait to get there so that I could pump water from the pump. We lived in Minneapolis and had what we called "running water," so it was exciting to pump water from the ground and carry it into Grandma's house. When we would visit other relatives on a farm nearby they would let me milk the cows, chop wood, and even crank up the old Model T. Many times my arms ached because they were so tired. But it was fun, and my arms became strong and firm.

Back in Minneapolis, I can remember shoveling snow, beating rugs, raking leaves, and washing clothes on a washboard. It was a real thrill to wait for the ice man to arrive with his horse-drawn wagon so that we could suck on a piece of ice while trying to help him carry the ice.

It seems that we were always moving and there was always something to do. We walked to the store, we walked to school, and we walked to the movies. Today we have snow plows, vacuum cleaners, automatic washing machines, refrigerators, dishwashers, etc. Automation has taken over. Everything is automatic, everything is geared to saving labor.

What all this is leading up to is that, in days past, "going to work" meant that you were going to do something that involved using your hands, arms, back, legs, or neck. Today, for the most part, it often means you are going to an office to sit at a desk, or in a meeting, or, in the evening or on a day off, to sit in front of a television set watching someone else get paid to work to entertain you.

As automation increased, we, as a nation, did less and less physically. Our children have grown up in the shadow of machines doing everything for them. We have developed a very large subspecies of Americans: "couch potatoes." Considering the number of couch potatoes in America, it is no wonder that as a nation, the physical fitness level of our children continues to drop to the point where, over the last two decades, it has slipped from one of the highest to one of the lowest in the world.

I am the first to admit that I love all the new labor-saving devices, but I feel it is essential that we get into a routine where we use our bodies as they were designed to be used: doing things physical.

Many people have become so "modernized" that they have completely forgotten the benefits of a more vigorous life. So, if everything is done for us and we are not using our muscles like we used to, something must be done to keep those muscles in good working order and that something is *body action*.

Well, you say, look at the statistics. There are more people than ever involved in physical fitness. That's correct. But compared to 20 years ago, there are more people overall, so more people involved in physical fitness doesn't necessarily raise the percentage of those who are physically fit. What this means is that more people than ever are *not into physical fitness.*

There are millions of people who have gone for years without being physically active, and who then decide to do something about overcoming inertia and aging. If you are one of these people who are now living life to the limit, and who is even more active than the younger generation, congratulations to you!

Then there is the other side of the coin, the growing number of people who are content to be inert. I can remember when I was on tour with my first book, *Fitness After 50*. I was in Texas doing a national cable call-in show. This lady called from Alaska after I had shown an exercise that is performed while sitting in a chair; it involves bringing the knees up to the chest. The woman from Alaska commented that she could not exercise because she could not bend her knees. I asked her if she could lift her leg up from the floor without bending it while sitting on the edge of the chair. I asked her to do it with me. She said she could, and I remarked that she had just done a leg-lift exercise. You see, you can work around your infirmities. But there are so many people who still believe that they cannot exercise and are content to sit around making excuses.

We have been brainwashed into believing in the modern way of always taking the path of least resistance. Have you ever seen a person drive into a shopping center parking lot on a perfectly gorgeous day, and drive up and down waiting for a parking place close to the entrance when there were many spaces open just 50 feet away? I've even done it myself. I became so modernized that I completely forgot the benefits of walking. Not any more, though.

The less you do, the less you want to do. It isn't time and aging that deteriorates the body. It's inertia or inactivity. Have you ever gone to a high school reunion and then looked back in your old yearbook? How do you look today compared to others at the reunion? How do you look compared to your picture in the yearbook? Have the sands of time shifted badly? You'll probably find that you and your friends who have remained active look much younger than those in your class who have not been active.

I'm certain you've known someone who has broken an arm. When the cast was removed, it looked withered and shriveled compared to the healthy arm. That arm probably started to atrophy as quickly as 90 minutes after the injury. When the arm was able to move again it gradually regained its original shape and muscle tone.

Activity, you see, is the archenemy of inertia.

While inactivity drains the vitality out of the muscles and produces atrophy, which results in listless and lifeless muscles, the opposite is true of activity.

Physical activity, first of all, causes more blood to be pumped to the muscles that are moving and working. The more blood being pumped to those muscles, the more oxygen and nutrients they are getting, making them better nourished and healthier. Secondly, the physical activity taking place within the muscle causes the muscle tissue to grow, become more flexible and have greater elasticity (the ability to return to its shape after it is flexed).

It's the old cliche: Use It Or Lose It.

If you don't use your muscles you're going to lose them. Another LaLannism I've heard Jack use time and time again is: "I'd rather wear out than rust out." The human body is such a wonderful machine. It only becomes stronger and better with use, while man-made machines eventually wear out from use.

Don't get discouraged if you haven't been physically active in years or even decades. The human muscle tissue is very regenerative in that it will begin to regain its elasticity, its strength, and its flexibility within weeks of your beginning a fitness program.

My uncle Bernard decided to change his lifestyle in his early 60s. He changed his dietary habits along with adding more physical activity, and today at 90 he says he doesn't have the aches and pains he did at 60 and feels wonderful.

Both Jack and I have known people who suddenly decided to take up a fitness program later in life and their only lament is that they didn't start a lot earlier to put their muscles back on the right track.

Just as that broken arm that had atrophied begins to come back to normal once it is put back into active service, so, too, can any muscle—or better yet, *all* your muscles—be brought back to life!

You've just got to want to do it.

THE PROCESS OF AGING

Aging is a process that the young can never envision and the old never seem to stop envisioning.

Where, then, is the cut-off point between being young and old? Well, I heard somewhere that we begin to walk the long road to old age the minute we are born. Perhaps that is true. But I believe that our rate of aging is measured not in years, but in how well our bodies hold up to the life through which they walk. The better we take care of our God-given bodies, the slower we age. The better our mental attitude toward life, the slower we age.

Some people are old when they are 25, while other people are young at 85. I can remember when my mother was 87. She said to me: "You know, Elaine, I really don't feel old. It's just that my feet don't want to go as fast anymore."

My uncle Bernard, who has lived in Guatemala City for over 40 years, is in his 90s. He continues to walk every day for exercise and is president of the American Club.

If you've ever watched "The Today Show," you've seen that more and more people who are living to be 100 and beyond are doing so by remaining active.

On the other hand, there are those people who decide that they are old at 60, or 50, or 40—or even 30!

For Americans, 65 seems to be the magic number because we've been brainwashed into thinking that 65 is the retirement age. The number 65 is an arbitrary one. Just because the government considers 65 retirement age, does this mean that when you hit 65 you've got to be physically and mentally older? Absolutely not!

We must look to what we have done to preserve our bodies, and we must look to what we can do to keep them healthy—and active.

If we expose a cell on our cheek to three hours of direct sunlight, that cell dries out, losing many properties that make it work efficiently. Nutrients do not move through the cell as well so it becomes stiff and undernourished; it is literally forced to age, and is often permanently damaged.

In point of fact, people who over-exposed their cells to the sun when they were young end up with skin that is withered and dried out like an old prune, and can often becomes cancerous.

Each cell in our body wages a daily war against the adversities we decide to throw at it.

Too much sun causes dryness and possibly skin cancer.

Too much cholesterol in the diet clogs arteries and this causes damage to the cells in the wall of the heart by depriving them of badly needed oxygen.

Too much alcohol can destroy cells in the liver and can cause cirrhosis of the liver. Alcohol also has a dehydrating effect upon the body, drying out cells and causing them to function at a fraction of their potential.

Smoking kills cells in the lungs and can ultimately lead to lung cancer. It also negatively affects the heart, the arteries, the skin, and various other body organs.

Too little exercise can cause the tone of the muscle cells to atrophy.

Failure to drink sufficient amounts of water each day causes the cells to become debilitated.

Go on a radical, trendy diet and the cells are denied necessary nourishment and become inefficient.

From the scientific side of things, some scientists consider aging a disease, much like measles or chicken pox, and they think that someday a cure will be found. Who knows? Someday a cure might be found for aging and all we will have to do to keep young will be to take a pill once a day or a shot once a year. Wouldn't that be something!

In the meantime, however, most of us aren't about to gamble that a cure will be found in our lifetimes. Our rate of aging is up to us. We can effect our own cure of sorts. This can be done by giving ourselves every chance to slow down the aging process by making sure our cells are bathed in oxygen from regular exercise, and by making certain our nutritional habits are in balance.

Scientists also tell us that when we look in the mirror and see the evidence of aging, it could be the end result of aging at a cellular level. Wrinkles, droopy skin under the chin, eyes, elbows, and arms, the loss of sparkle in the eyes, and the loss of a certain amount of get-up-and-go is an apparent demonstration of aging in our collective cells.

We must always appreciate the fact that the human body is composed of billions of individual cells working together in different body systems to create the total organism: the human being. It is all of these systems working together that create life itself, and that allow the human being to move, to process food—even to think.

Cells are continually replacing themselves and are dependent for their health on having their basic needs met.

You can plainly see that what we do to our cells, and to our various body systems, we ultimately do to ourselves. If our cells are not given proper rest, are not given adequate exercise, are not oxygenated and fed properly, they will be of inferior quality. And since the billions of cells that make up our body are continually rebuilding themselves, doesn't it stand to reason that if we exercise and feed our bodies properly, we will become more efficient overall?

Exercise speeds up the process of getting rid of dead cells and replacing them with new, fresh cells. As long as it is done scientifically, exercise increases the ability of the cells to function, promotes the transport of oxygen and nutrients to the cells, and makes them stronger and more enduring. Various body systems will respond to the increased exercise applied specificially to them.

A muscle is made up of millions of tiny little cells and the more resistance you give to that muscle on behalf of those cells, the more strength and energy you develop. Let me give you an example. Put your right hand straight out in front of you. Now use your right hand to touch your right shoulder, bending at the elbow. Do this three or four times. Now make a tight fist and bring that fist up slowly, continually squeezing it. With your left hand feel the bicep muscle in your right arm as you make these movements. You should be able to feel a muscle flexing. The same thing happens when we use a weight; the weight, however, produces more resistance, and resistance is the key to getting the job done faster.

When we exercise, all systems of the body benefit to some extent, but it's the parts of the body that we specifically work on that tend to improve to a much greater degree. And this improvement goes right down to the cellular level, where aging occurs.

It's up to us to help retard aging. Our body cells are willing to do their part, but we have to be willing to do our part to help them help us.

WHY SOME BODY PARTS ATROPHY

I looked up the word "atrophy" in Blackiston's Medical Dictionary and found the first definition: "a reduction in size of an organ or cell which previously reached a larger size." I was amazed to find a page and a half of explanations having to do with cells. Everything from muscular, heart, liver, brain, to optic nerves, bones, and face. As I read on under *degenerative* and *disuse* the book states that "a form in which cellular degeneration is conspicuous . . . that form resulting from inactivity, usually affecting glandular or muscular structures. Also called inactivity." Whew! That was a long way around to find out the simple fact that inactivity equals atrophy.

When my husband Jack was in his senior year in high school, playing in his last football game at Berkeley High School in the early 1930s, he sustained a severe knee injury. He was given one of the first knee operations, but was told that he would probably never walk again. He was in a cast and on crutches for three months. When the cast was removed, atrophy had taken place, and his leg was shrunken and withered.

All through school, Jack had studied Gray's Anatomy. He knew his stuff. The local policemen and firemen used to work out in his backyard by using equipment he had invented. He built those guys up and tore them down to rebuild them through a discipline of exercise and proper nutrition. He kept records on the progress of each of those men. His records were not unlike those a scientist uses when doing research for a thesis.

He was convinced that his advanced knowledge of kinesiology would enable him to rehabilitate the knee and prove the doctors wrong. He determined that he would walk again. Little by little he began to put more pressure on his leg. He began a strenuous exerise program, even though the pain was excruciating. He began a series of daily exercises for the thighs on a machine of his own design. The machine is today known as a legextension machine.

There is a street in Berkeley named Marin. It is one of the steepest streets in the Bay Area: straight up almost a mile. Jack's goal was to walk to the top. He started at the bottom and every day he would increase a few more steps until one day he finally reached the top. His leg had filled out, and his muscle tone had returned, and he had reached his goal!

In 1980, while driving his car, Jack was hit head-on by a truck that had lost control in the rain while it was coming down a hill near our house. Jack's "good" knee was smashed into the dashboard and was badly injured. After an operation on that knee, the doctors got him up and moving around immediately because today they know that atrophy begins to set in about 90 minutes after an injury.

I didn't have to have something as traumatic as an operation to notice atrophy taking place in my body.

I have a photograph of myself when I was 19. I was really in good shape from swimming in the Minneapolis Aqua Follies.

Some eight years after that picture was taken, I began to notice that the inner part of my thighs were not as full. Standing with my legs together, I could not get the thighs to touch each other. I actually lost inches around them. I was also losing inches around my chest, yet my stomach was getting larger. It seems as though my chestline was sinking into my waistline.

I went on an exercise program and concentrated on exercises that would build my inner thighs and chest. I also did exercises that would strengthen my stomach muscles and within a short time I saw improvements. A transformation had taken place. I had managed to counter atrophy.

Maybe some of you have noticed similar changes in your bodies. You, too, can reshape and remold your body if you desire to do so. When Jack and I are on a lecture tour or on radio and television call-in shows, questions on what to do with those troublesome spots always come up. We'll get into that later in the book, but for now, let's think about how changes come about.

We know for certain that one of the major factors is inactivity. Remember that I mentioned before that fat is like a river. It will go to the spot where there is the least resistance.

For example, do you know someone who has spent most of their lives sitting in a chair, whether it is at home or in an office? The very real evidence of those years spent sitting usually develops into a broadening of the "old back porch." What caused the posterior spread? Lack of activity and probably gravity.

Gravity acted upon an increasingly weak body structure and upon the vertebrae of the backbone. From lack of stretching, exercise, and most likely from poor posture, gravity began to compress the spine, pressing down on one vertebrae after the other from the constant pressure of supporting the upper body. As the vertebrae compress, the vital organs inside the body also become compressed and lead to all sorts of internal problems.

An interesting fact to note here is that the measured pressure inside the vertebrae disc is much higher when sitting than while standing. It is important to be aware of the fact that if the muscles involved in sitting are not kept well-toned, as the vertebrae compresses, it may not be able to resist the slow work or erosion.

I refer to it as "slow erosion" because it is a process that occurs in many aspects of nature when there is no resistance. The Appalachian Mountains are only a few thousand feet high, but at one time they were as high as the Rocky Mountains: 10,000 feet or more. But over tens of thousands of years, many thousands of rainstorms and the grinding of glaciers combined to erode them down to what they are today. It can work the same way with the human body. The force of gravity does not change; the body's ability to resist it changes.

Later in this book, we'll discuss in more detail how we can fight gravity and return certain body parts to good working order. And at the same time, besides those body parts being more functional, they'll also look better.

Chapter 2

Reversing The Years That Worked Against You

When some of my friends found out I was writing a book on improving specific body parts, they asked me to go into some of the troublesome areas that plague women and men. Do men and women have different problem zones? Do they *need* different exercises for different parts of the body?

Overall physical conditioning works the same for men as it does for women, but men and women tend to accumulate fat in different places. Let's look at some of those places:

1. Hips. The hips, to a large extent, are determined by the size of the pelvic bones. The female pelvis is generally wider than a man's because of her capacity to bear children. This is an area fraught with frustration for most women because it seems that fat likes to take up residence there, and women, by nature, have more body fat than men to begin with. (Men tend to have more muscle mass in the hip area.) When that area is not exercised properly it cannot hold up its end of the fight against gravity, and the flesh tends to hang and sag toward the ground. Some jokingly refer to this condition as "saddlebags."

If you have studied art, you will recall that several centuries ago a woman who had rather small features from the navel up but who was disproportionately wide in the hips and thighs was con-

sidered beautiful. You'll see this in such paintings as The Turkish Bath (1859-62) by Ingres and even Renoir's The Bathers (1884-87). Unfortunately, the 18th and 19th century populace did not have the advantage of knowing that such excessive body fat can lead to a great number of health problems. But then, due to the prominence of fatal diseases, many overfat people didn't live long enough for their excess fat to contribute to their deaths. Today we know that excessive fat poses not only a health problem, but can be a psychological problem as well. Excessive hip weight also contributes to difficulty in mobility. The more difficult it is to move, the less likely one is going to move, and the more excessive the hips will become.

The male doesn't seem to share these problems with women unless he is grossly overfat.

2. Thighs. Overly large thighs are often linked to overly large hips, but not in all cases. It should be understood that the largest *muscles* in the body are in the thighs. The thighs were made to do a great deal of the body's work, specifically to move the body by either walking or running. Unfortunately, they are also a depository for fat on some women. Fortunately, since the thighs *do* contain the human body's largest muscles, they are capable of burning up an inordinate amount of body fat once they are trained to exercise.

3. Underdeveloped arms and shoulders. How many women have you heard over the years say that it's impossible to do even one push-up or one chin-up? Quite a few, right? In our world of modern conveniences, the upper body of the female is typically underdeveloped. (You will notice that this is not true of the women who play tennis or swim regularly.) As we mentioned above, many women have very small (and undeveloped) upper bodies and wide lower bodies. One way of making a body more well-proportioned (which is the emphasis of this book) is to burn off excess fat; but another way is to develop some muscle tone. For the woman with an underdeveloped upper body, a few choice exercises practiced regularly will yield startling results. I've worked with women who claimed to be unable to do one push-up but who, after six weeks, could do a half-dozen, and who, once they had, tended to get in little extra workouts every once in a while to show off just how well they *could* do them. The basic push-up (done in the female format, with knees on the floor), as we will see later, can do wonders for defining the upper arms and shoulders. There are also a half-dozen other simple exercises that can contribute to making your body more proportionate and stronger, but without developing bulging muscles.

And let's not forget the men. At one time, when most male jobs involved a lot of lifting, carrying, throwing, and swinging, the upper bodies were well-developed and well-muscled. With today's office jobs, the typical male will be lucky to have to carry a pile of papers from one desk to another. Men are fortunate, however, because due to their larger proportion of muscle to fat tissue, workouts designed to develop muscle tone and muscle definition will typically show up faster than on a female.

4. Bra-strap overhang. Okay, here's one that most men get out of. This is a particularly annoying problem, especially so for women, although surprisingly enough, some men do exhibit this problem, especially if they are overfat. For women, the fat tends to hang over the bra straps. For men, the flesh droops just below the underarms in the area of the latissimus dorsi, which is located on the outside of the shoulder blades.

5. Double chin, jowls, and/or turkey neck. This is an area where men and women have something in common. Excessive fat around the neck can take the form of a double or triple chin.

Cheeks that have fallen to fat and gravity are often called jowls, and the hanging and drooping flesh around the neck (sometimes called turkey neck) is due to either poor muscle tone or to someone going on a crash diet and not exercising that area. These conditions can be improved if we concentrate on fat loss and muscle tone build-up simultaneously.

6. Pot belly, etc. Most men want to know what to do about their "beer belly" or "belt buckle overhang." Some refer to it as their "blubber gut." Women tend to ask questions about their "protruding stomach," "pot belly," or that "pregnant look." You may recall that Jack used to refer to it on his television program as the "front porch." No matter what you call it, it is one of the biggest problems most people face. This problem doesn't just strike older people. You see it on teenagers, middle-agers and old-agers as well.

There is a structure inside the body called the omentum. It is attached to the stomach and serves as an internal apron that covers the intestines. It more or less acts as a protection and supporting framework for the internal organs. It is placed within and behind the muscles that underlie the skin of the abdomen and has a great capacity to store fat. As the fat grows, the omentum swells and spreads out and so does the abdomen. It does seem logical that if we keep our stomach muscles working and watch what we put into our mouths, the omentum would store less fat and would hold up better. We'll get into exercises for the stomach later in the book.

7. Love handles. The folds of skin that frequently form on the sides of the waist are related to the expanded abdomen. Since the male hips are not proportionately as wide as the female's, when excess fat forms, the fat does not tend to blend with the hips. Instead, it becomes more prominent. This is what some people call their spare tire, or as we said earlier, "love handles." Again, we need more action in that area to correct the problem.

But don't despair. It is never too late to start work on these areas. So let's think in terms of pacing ourselves for long-term results.

To help reverse those years that have worked against us, we must change the habits that got us into the condition we're in now. We are the sum total of our habits. To change them around, we must do just the opposite of what we have been used to doing.

But we *can* do it, and we *will* do it.

Chapter 3

Time Is Still On Your Side

The human body is a miracle of resiliency. It is not only ready, but anxious to bounce back from adversity. Medical research indicates that a person who has smoked for twenty years can have most of the useful function of the lungs return within two years after giving up cigarettes.

In more personal terms, I'm reminded of Walter Stack of San Francisco who, as this book is written, is in his 80s. He decided to take up running when he was in his sixties and subsequently ran more than 100 marathons, ran the grueling Western States 100, and competed in the Hawaii Ironman Triathlon. He didn't breathe down the neck of the winner in each event, but he paced himself, and he successfully completed the races.

This is not to say that people over 50 should emulate Walter Stack and go out and run a marathon every other week. But people like Walter can certainly serve as inspirations to all of us; they prove that almost anything is possible, that it's never too late.

Or how about Alan Burgoyne of Australia who began running at 61, and who now holds the record in the 70-75 year age group in the 10,000 meters with an astonishing 40:40 time? Burgoyne competes in the World Veteran Championships and over the past three competitions won four golds, two silvers and three bronze medals.

Or how about Lary Webster who is 52 and won the Mt. Si Marathon in Washington state with a 2:47:28.

Or 70-year-old Marcie Trent of Anchorage, who ran a 26-mile marathon in Napa Valley in March 1988 in 4 hours and 11 minutes!

There are numerous examples of people who got into exercise relatively late in life, paced themselves in getting fit, and who accomplished the seemingly impossible. Almost anyone, at any age, can get fit, stay fit and by doing so, change their lives for the better.

Keep these basic points in mind:

1. Have a complete physical, including stress test. This will give you a base line from which to begin. It will give you an idea of where you are, what you are capable of, and the speed at which you should progress. Perhaps the most fun that comes from a physical is to have a yardstick against which you can measure yourself. Having a complete physical with stress test will give you the data you need to measure your progress. Then, each year, as you are retested and continue your fitness plan, you should see some startling changes. In many instances, these changes will be an indication that you're becoming healthier.

2. Decide just what you want from a fit lifestyle. Is it better endurance, more energy reserves, weight control, better overall health? Do you want to look and feel better? Is there a sport you've always wanted to try but were always too unfit to take up? Would you like to become more flexible as other people your age become stiff in the joints? Or perhaps there is a little of each of these reasons behind your motivation. There is absolutely nothing wrong if your reasons for getting fit include a bit of all the above. It is good, before you start, to have evaluated, in your own head, your reasons for putting in the time and effort to build a better body. Knowing why you're doing it in the first place will keep you motivated.

3. Begin with a very simple, basic fitness program. For this, I recommend *Fitness After 50*, a book I wrote to help mature people get into a regular fitness program without overdoing it. (Or, you can begin by using a regular walking program. See my book *Dynastride!*) The important thing is to begin slowly. The quickest way to discourage yourself is to take on too much at one time. If you do take on too much at one time you can become sore or tired or discouraged and you'll become turned off to fitness. Start easy and pace yourself well and you'll be astonished at the positive changes. (For those who feel compelled to begin their body parts program without the advantage of a fitness base, directions are included.)

4. Branch out from the basic fitness plateau into specific areas. This includes improving various specific body parts (the emphasis of this book) and it also includes becoming involved in specific sports, especially those of an aerobic nature. Since you are working so hard to get fit, you might as well end up being able to have fun with your fitness, whether it's being able to swim, walk the golf course, play tennis, or hop on a bicycle. Make your fitness translate into something that's fun in your life.

5. Never say never. I'm always reminded of how many children I know who love the story of the little locomotive that said "I can!" The story is an inspiration to children, and in situations where I'm faced with a little obstacle to overcome, I often find myself recalling that very simple story. Never say never. Instead, say "I can do it! I will do it!" Developing this attitude will help keep you fit and will help keep you improving, but it also has so many wonderful applications to other aspects of life. Remember: "Yes, I *can* do it!"

Remember that it is never too late to get fit. With fitness, you always get back what you put into it—with interest.

And don't be afraid to pick out a hero or heroine. Use the exploits of people like Walt Stack, Alan Burgoyne, Lary Webster, and Marcie Trent to inspire you. I use my husband, Jack, as my inspiration. Keep at it, and who knows? *You* may become someone else's inspiration!

ONE STEP AT A TIME TO A NEW YOU

As I write this, I have recently returned from Detroit, where I lectured at a convention. After I had finished speaking, a lovely lady who was overly fat by 20-25 pounds came up to me and told me she was inspired to try to remold her body but felt it was just an impossibility at her age. I attempted to continue the encouragement theme of my lecture by saying things like "It's never too late" and "Anything in life is possible if you believe it." When we got to talking about age, she perked up when she learned that we were both born in the year 1926. With a glimmer of hope, she asked: "Do you think my body could ever look like yours?" I answered: "Why not?"

I told her that I believed that it could, but that she would have to believe it, too. I prevailed upon her not to think about how difficult it was going to be to accomplish her goal, but rather to take it one day at a time. She left filled with enthusiasm and ready to start immediately on all the suggestions I had given in my lecture regarding "Problem Zones of the Body." (I want to share these suggestions with you, too; that's really why I have written this book.)

No matter what we contemplate, it appears to be a herculean task when we concentrate on the finished result. We should be considering the challenge one step at a time. For instance, if I asked you to tear the Manhattan telephone directory in half, could you do it? Of course not. It seems impossible. However, if you just tear out one page at a time until you get to the middle, you will have torn the telephone book in half. That seemingly impossible, herculean task became simple when you changed your approach to it. So anything is possible if you know how.

Without further ado, let's pick out the top five areas you're interested in improving.

To help you get going, let me pick the one body part that I think is number 1. Then you can fill in numbers 2, 3, 4 and 5.

1. The Heart. From a physical standpoint, the heart should always come first. It is the key. If it is weak, your entire body is weak. Fortunately, as a muscle, the heart is quite capable of growing stronger. And, the way aerobic exercise works, as the heart is strengthened, so are the lungs and so is the circulatory system. And—Bonus!—so are a multitude of other systems. The easiest way to start the heart working to build and improve itself is simply to walk. Walk every day that you can. Not too much too soon. But a little one day and a little the next day will make you capable of more and more, and in no time at all you'll be walking distances you once thought impossible. A good walking program has other terrific side effects. Besides strengthening the heart so you can expand into other areas, it also builds up and strengthens the legs. And from there you can progress to jogging and running and bicycle riding and swimming. Get into the habit of walking—and continue walking for the rest of your life. And as you become stronger, do it with more and more vigor! Besides building up the heart, walking also burns calories (which contributes to fat loss). Walking one mile in 20 minutes burns up 72 calories; walking one mile in 15 minutes burns 95 calories, and walking one mile in 12 minutes burns up 128 calories, which is roughly the same as running one mile.

So, get the heart strong and you'll be able to move directly into your four priority areas, getting them under control one at a time. Your largest deficiency area should come first. Then go on to other problem zones, listing them in order of priority. One way to find out what your deficiencies are is to take off all your clothes and look at yourself in a full-length mirror. So now, in order of priority, write in your problem zones:

2. _____
3. _____
4. _____
5. _____

MAKING GOOD USE OF YOUR TIME

You've already started your program because at the end of the last section, you made the decision to shape up certain body parts by putting together the priority list that commenced with the top priority of the heart.

When you consider it from this perspective, you have already done quite a bit.

The only consideration left is to set a logical date on which to begin.

Some people like to tie their start with days that are special to them, such as a birthday, a wedding anniversary, or on some holiday, such as Independence Day, on which they can declare independence from the grip of inertia.

For others, much revolves around the first day of the week, or the first day of the month. The first of the month, or the first week of the month becomes even more of a factor later in the book when we get down to Total Body Programs based on a 30-day cycle.

There is no time like the present to start. There are those of you who can't see wasting time sitting around waiting for the first of the month or the first week of the month or the next great holiday and find no better day for starting a project than Today. To those who refuse to put off until tomorrow what you can do today, I say, *More power to you. Go for it!*

MEDICAL CONSULTATION

We've already discussed the necessity of anyone who is about to embark on a fitness program getting a complete physical with stress test. It gives you a scientific evaluation of your condition on many different levels. And it may also uncover any impending problem areas, many of which could possibly be improved with an exercise program, but must be watched carefully in order to avoid medical complications.

It should be mentioned at this point that the doctor you consult on the initial medical evaluation should be a person who is familiar with the current research on exercise and with the benefits of exercise for the mature person. Evaluate your doctor just as thoroughly as he is going to evaluate you. Although smoking cigarettes among medical students is almost nonexistent today, some doctors still smoke. I wouldn't presume you would want to receive advice from a doctor who is overfat and who sits in his office smoking.

You are entitled to shop around for a doctor who is going to be interested in your fitness program, and if he looks fit, you're going to have more confidence in him or her.

If after examining you, your doctor feels there are some areas that should be precluded and feels that an exercise program would not be advisable at this time, be sure you obtain an adequate explanation. If you don't understand what your doctor is telling you, ask again. You are entitled to a satisfactory explanation of any restriction put on your physical activity or any impending problems that might occur. If you don't feel you've received a satisfactory explanation, you might want to seek a second opinion.

Your condition may be a passing one or may be correctable so that you can ultimately take up an exercise program once the condition is corrected.

That is why I would advise a person just beginning a progressive exercise program to schedule a check-up with the doctor. That is why periodic check-ups, say every six months, are advisable.

A periodic check-up is like a regular progress report. It can measure the condition of your body and maximize the good things you are doing for it.

Your doctor can track the positive changes in everything from pulse rate to body fat to blood pressure to cholesterol level. A person involved in exercise may, after the first three months, *feel* vastly improved, yet may not be convinced that real progress has been made. The medical examination will give solid medical proof, in numbers and data, that the hours of exercise are producing a beneficial effect. This can be a great motivator.

Remember that once you become fit, instead of being apprehensive and fearing what a physical examination might reveal, you'll begin to look forward to seeing scientific proof of the progress you feel you have made.

THE TIDE TURNS IN YOUR FAVOR

The fact that you want to reshape and redesign your body is an indication that the tide is turning in your favor. You have made a commitment to yourself and now you can look forward to getting specific results in specific areas. Two common questions seem to crop up when the decision to remold the body is made:

1. Do I do my exercise program alone or with others?
2. Where should I do my exercising?

Let's deal with question No. 1 first.

Should you plan your workouts alone or with others? Yes, and no. What do you prefer? What lifestyle do you currently follow? Are you self-conscious about your body at the moment and want to keep it under wraps until it begins to make its changes for the better? Are you the type person who needs to do workouts with friends in order to stay motivated? Let's discuss each option:

Solo: Some people love the serenity of exercising alone. It allows them to think and to solve problems and to become more intimately acquainted with the workings of their wonderfully complex bodies. I asked Jack why he generally works out alone. "I have in the past worked out with a partner, but it was someone close to my capabilities who was as enthusiastic and sincere as I was about working out. That was why we could help and encourage each other. Today it is difficult to find someone who has all those qualities, so I would rather work out alone so I can concentrate on every movement I'm doing." This tendency to want to be alone is especially true of exercisers who have a long history of enjoying aerobic sports, such as distance swimming, long-distance running, or using home gym type aerobic exercise devices. It is not quite so common among aerobic exercisers such as bicyclists, walkers/hikers, and cross-country skiers.

With a Partner: Other people find that they can best be motivated by exercising with another person on a regular basis. This "buddy system" works especially well for people who are not as self-motivated and for those who are uncomfortable with doing things alone. It is an excellent way to provide motivation, but it can be discouraging if the one partner begins to show progress before the other. This is the time when the partner who *is* showing progress must come to his or her friend's aid by encouraging the other to keep with it. It should also be remembered when training with a partner that the less fit of the two should be the yardstick for how much work is done in unison; the weaker should not be forced to keep up with the stronger or it will become too discouraging. The partner method works especially well with aerobic sports such as bicycling, walking/hiking and cross-country skiing, and also works very well with calisthenic-type exercising. Jack has some good observations about how the buddy system *can* work. "A lot of people don't like to work out alone. They like to work out with a partner. When I started my gym, I did everything I could possibly do to get people to enjoy their workouts. I would get the people in the gym who were physically evenly matched, and keep them working out together, using self-resistance. We'd use towels as the tool. One person would grab the towel while the other would resist. Then they would change roles. It worked just like a weight workout—as long as the two partners were comparable in strength."

In a Group: This, of course, is the basis of virtually all aerobic dance. The group approach is wonderful for people who find the almost party-like atmosphere motivating and enticing, and is also wonderful for the person who is a little self-conscious because with this method, he or she can blend in with the group instead of standing out. Of course, there are drawbacks: there is less individual attention given, you are more structured as far as times when the exercises are done, and the individual often tries to keep up with the group even though he or she may not be at that specific level at that time. On the plus side, of course, is the camaraderie and the excellent motivational aspect. The group approach is also terrific because for many people it gives them several times in a week when they have set aside time for themselves. Of course, the group approach does not work well where certain types of exercising are involved. I've also known groups of women who organized to get together in each others' homes several times a week to do exercises but found that there was a tendency, without a strong leader, to have the sessions slip into more chatter than exercise.

The Combo Approach: Try all these approaches. Work out alone. Try working out with a partner. Try working out with a group. There is something good to say about all three ways. Mix it up. Variety keeps exercising from becoming boring.

As to the question of *where* you exercise, the options are even greater!

A Gym or Spa: Again, it is a matter of preference. A gym or spa is probably the ultimate place for a workout. There are so many high-tech pieces of equipment today. Some of them even talk to you to tell you whether you are doing the exercise correctly. Using this equipment gives you the opportunity to change the resistance to fit your needs. Spas and gyms also have qualified instructors and certified aerobics instructors to help you to your goal. YMCAs and YWCAs also offer aerobic dance classes and other exercise classes, and if you like to work out with a group, this is the place for you. Additionally, after working out, most gyms and spas have all of the luxury items (sauna baths, steam rooms, massage experts, etc.) where you can indulge yourself with the full treatment in reward for doing a good workout.

Your Home or a Friend's Home: Many people can't get out or can't afford to go to a spa, but prefer to work out at home or at a friend's house. Home exercise equipment is also available for those who can afford it. It can run from as little as $50 to as much as a small automobile. Maybe you prefer to keep it simple. If you want to keep things very simple, you'll find that most of the exercises included in *Fitness After 50* and in this book can be done either with no hardware or with simple things you'll find around the house. It is best if you are going to exercise at home to set a spot aside so that there is a feeling of sameness and regularity that accompanies the workouts. The space does not have to be large and it does not have to be monopolized by exercise equipment when it is not being used. Virtually any place will work: a corner of the garage or basement, the utility or family room, or the center of the living room. It is helpful to have an exercise mat that you can put down in order to provide a comfortable surface. Most mats are inexpensive, fold up neatly and easily for storage, and make a world of difference. There's nothing more difficult than trying to work out on a hardwood floor—especially in the winter when it is both hard *and* chilly.

The Great Outdoors: When the weather is nice, open all your windows. Or try exercising outdoors. Perhaps a spot in your backyard or on the roof of your apartment building. There's nothing like exercising in the open air. Certainly, most of the aerobic exercising I encourage—walking, running, swimming, skiing, bicycling—is done outside, but when the weather does not permit, there are indoor machines that almost duplicate every one of the aerobic exercises, plus there are certainly plenty of indoor pools for swimming all year long.

It doesn't matter who you do or don't exercise with, but it's important to have a special place where you exercise. By being creative and by keeping your exercising fresh and varied, you'll want to schedule some exercising in almost every environment you can think of.

Remember that there are no set rules. It's a personal preference. Just so you *do* exercise.

SPECIAL CLOTHING

No matter what kind of activity you do, there is

an outfit made for you that will make you feel not only comfortable, but stylish and sleek.

We live at a point in time when exercise clothing has nearly reached a peak of perfection. During the past several years exercise clothing has taken huge steps in both style/design and functionality. The increasing demand for this activewear fueled both the domestic and foreign markets, and manufacturers stepped in to respond to the need.

New materials that breathe and move with the exercising body as though they were a second skin have been developed. There are startling new colors and incredible combinations. New materials have been developed so that a triathlete can swim, bike and run in the same outfit. Fabrics have been made thinner and more flexible so that cross-country skiers, hikers, bicyclists and runners can continue training in the worst of weather.

You don't really need something fashionable and designer-inspired to help you work out; anything you can find in your wardrobe will do as long as it's comfortable.

I do my workouts in two or three outfits that are comfortable yet stylish.

Often I will work out in an old hand-me-down sweatsuit that my son Jon Allen discarded (even though it wasn't really that old). I dearly love that sweatsuit because it's so comfortable and warm on cold days. I feel all snuggly in it. But after my workout, I'll change into some of the latest activewear, which I then tend to wear for the rest of the day. It looks much more stylish.

I guess I'm like everyone else: I like to keep up with the latest styles.

Jack likes to work out in sweatsuits because they help absorb perspiration. For years he has worked out in old gray sweatsuits, but the past 10 years or so, Hattie Montez, our housekeeper for 30 years (now retired; she has worked for Jack for over 40 years), told him he needed more colors, so every Christmas she buys him sweatsuits in different colors. At present, he has red, white, blue, and yellow sweats. Most serious exercisers in any sport don't care what they wear, as long as it is comfortable.

A runner or walker tends to work out in simple race T-shirts, of which he or she has a drawerful. A bicyclist may use the same top both winter and summer because it is of a material that cools in the summer and warms in the winter. Swimmers may have two or three different suits, but if they are serious, the suits are usually more functional than fashionable.

Women who take aerobic dance classes seem to be very fashionable, although some of the women in the classes are more practical, using simple gray sweatsuits, in an attempt to play down their figure until they've managed to get it into a little better shape.

When choosing clothes for exercise, choose clothing specifically to accommodate and ease you through your exercise.

For most aerobic sports (with the exception of swimming and cross-country skiing), you can use pretty much the same outfit. Women would do well to investigate an athletic bra, such as a Jog-Bra®

Your simplest exercise clothes will be adequate for the exercises outlined in this book, as well as for the exercises in *Fitness After 50*.

The area of clothing you *should* be most concerned with is footwear.

If you are going to engage in aerobic sports at a basic fitness and recreational level, a good, stable pair of running shoes could cover you for walking, jogging/running, bicycling, rope-jumping, etc.

If your aerobic base is being provided by aerobic dance, however, you should invest in a suitable pair of aerobic shoes. Running shoes are not very good for aerobic dance because the running shoes do not provide lateral support, as the aerobic shoes do.

I would recommend that a person doing aerobic dance *always* wear good aerobics shoes, especially as you get older. The feet and ankles need support. Doing aerobic dance and/or exercises (as outlined in this book) without shoes *can* put unnecessary stress and strain on the arches, the soles, the heels and the ankles. Also, in many instances, the aerobic shoes will grip better on the floor, whether it's the floor of your bedroom or family room or the floor of the local gym or spa.

No matter what your exercise routines, it is important to take good care of your feet.

The developments in running shoes over the past decade have been a real boon to us (a.k.a. recycled teenagers). The shoes are lightweight, offer plenty of support and impact protection, and have made significant contributions toward allowing older people to walk farther with less discomfort than ever before.

It would be worth your while to invest in at least one good pair of running or aerobic shoes. Your feet will thank you.

PART TWO

The Body Part Specific Program

Chapter 4

How To Begin

STEP ONE

When I think of step one, I think of a baby who has become proficient in crawling and is trying to begin to walk. The uncertainty of the unknown is overwhelming and frightening. But once the first step is taken, one can appreciate the sense of accomplishment. The apprehension is lifted, it's fun, and before long the infant is into everything.

If you've ever started on a new job or changed jobs, even in your own field, the new surroundings, policies, and management are all somewhat awesome. But once you get into the swing of things, it becomes familiar to you and before you know it, you have settled into a routine. That is what I want you to do with this book: settle into a routine.

Many of you have built up a fitness base and have increased your strength, flexibility, and endurance by doing a general workout (as prescribed in my book *Fitness After 50*) or in a program based on aerobic fitness augmented by strength and flexibility exercises as Warm-Up and Cool-Downs (as presented in my second book, *Dynastride!*).

The Body Specific Program that follows is done to augment—not as a substitute for—the general fitness program you are already following. (Part III will bring all your programs together into one.) I suggest you start out doing this Body Part Specific program three days a week. (If you are currently not involved in a fitness program, but want to begin this program, do not attempt to do it more than three days a week, making certain to schedule an off-day between exercise days.) On the days you do your Body Part Specific workout, exclude your regular fitness program. For instance, if you are involved in a vigorous walking program three days a week, add the Body Part Specific program on the other three days. For example:

Sunday—Free Day
Monday—Walk
Tuesday—Body Parts Exercise
Wednesday—Walk
Thursday—Body Parts Exercise
Friday—Walk
Saturday—Body Parts Exercise

This schedule allows you to not only continue your base program (in this case walking) but also increase your activity through the Body Specific Program aimed directly at the body part(s) that concern you. I feel it is important to keep at least one rest day at first. Your rest day is also your "reward day." I call it my R'n'R Day—Rest and Reward. It is your reward, your bonus, for increasing your activity and sticking with it. It also gives your muscles a chance to recuperate. As you become stronger, you can either increase your repetitions in the Body Parts Exercise, add an additional body part, or add a Walk day in the place of a Free Day. (Much later in this program, there will be several days a week when you'll not only walk but do body parts exercises as well.)

No matter what exercise program you decide on, whether it concentrates on a specific body part or whether it is to just become more reasonably fit, it's best to have a foundation of basic fitness. Just as you wouldn't erect the roof or the walls of a new house until the foundation was finished, you shouldn't work on specific body parts until you enjoy some basic fitness.

Basic fitness can be achieved by a regular program of aerobic dance or by a vigorous walking program or by a combination. What is important is that you regularly raise your pulse rate for 20 minutes or more and that you and your body are comfortable with at least a modest level of exercise.

STEP TWO

Some people are extremely talented in being able to do just about anything after being told only once how to do it. Occasionally there's something I can get on the first try, but I prefer if someone walks me through it or shows me how to do it the first time.

So if you don't mind my coming along on your first day's exercise with you, I'll walk you through it.

The step we'll concentrate on now is a mental step. Let's call it Clearing the Mind.

So before you begin your exercise program for the day, try these few suggestions:
1. Decide on your exercise program for the day.
2. Relax. Take a deep breath through your nose and exhale through your mouth. (Remember the Dynamic Breathing that Jack used to do on his TV show?)
3. Weed out and discard all negative thoughts, concerns, and pressing problems from your mind.
4. Begin filling the open space in your mind with calmness and positive thoughts.
5. Imagine you are about to refuel and refill your body with energy.
6. Visualize yourself going smoothly through your exercise routine.

Visualization is a process that many professional athletes go through before an important game or competition. They visualize themselves going through certain important plays, moving through certain physical ranges of motion impor-

THESE FEET WERE MADE FOR WALKING— Despite several very serious knee injuries during various phases of his life, Jack likes to join Elaine on her daily walks near their home in Morro Bay. The LaLannes believe in positive physical solutions to a variety of life's problems, both physical and psychological.

tant to their performance. This is a method that is successfully employed by everyone from world-renowned ballet dancers to tackles on professional football teams, from Olympic high jumpers to amateur triathletes.

The unknown is frightening to people. Visualization is a method to make the unknown known.

By visualizing yourself doing your routine in advance, your mind will have already been through it several times and your body will know better what it is expected to do.

If you've given yourself enough time to empty your head of non-exercise things and to fill your mind with positive feelings and well-orchestrated versions of your upcoming workout, you can expand the scene to include every detail, from changing into your exercising clothes to taking a shower afterwards.

I use visualization in many things I do in life, including my golf game. Before a tournament (if it's on a course with which I am familiar), I visualize and see myself successfully completing each hole to my capabilities and satisfaction. I say to my capabilities and satisfaction because I'm not a par golfer.

If it is a course with which I am not familiar, I still visualize myself successfully using all of my golf clubs satisfactorily, including chipping and putting.

Now imagine yourself getting dressed in your exercise clothing. Be specific. Pick out the exact clothing you want to wear. Something that is comfortable and loose-fitting.

Now walk slowly and purposefully to the space that you have set aside for your exercising. Remember that this is *your* space. It has no other purpose in the universe but to be your space. Of all the zillions of square feet in the universe, these several square feet are intimately and totally yours.

Begin by sitting quietly in your exercise space for one minute and 40 seconds. One hundred seconds. Sit down in whatever position is most comfortable. Close your eyes, count slowly to 100 and while you're counting, again go through your workout in your mind. You needn't go through every repetition. Just skim through it. Hit every exercise, but if you feel intimately comfortable with each exercise, do them only one time each in your head.

If you reach 100 and are not yet finished with your routine, give yourself 20 more seconds and finish up mentally.

Now, you are set to begin.

STEP THREE

Every exercise session should consist of three parts: Warm-Up, the heart of the session, and the Cool-Down.

You have already picked your priority body parts. (See page 14.) Remember: start with your first priority body part and work on it until you feel some progress is being made. Then add your next body part. When the second body part begins to show progress, add a third. And so forth.

To make this process easier, there are exercise forms included directly after this discussion. They are there to assist you in keeping track of your workouts. Make copies of them as needed and keep them in a 3-ring binder.

You will notice that space for the Warm-Up and Cool-Down exercises are already included; these should be done before and after each session. For the Warm-Up and Cool-Down exercises, you can pick a selection from virtually any exercise book (*Dynastride!* contains a complete program) or you can use exercises from your aerobics class or create a set of your own that stretch and loosen

your muscles.

Remember that your heart is your most important body part, but it is already being used successfully by your involvement in a general fitness program. So now take your top priority body part (see page 14) and fill it in where it says Body Part at the top of the chart. Now, pick out the exercises for that particular body part in the exercise section (pp. 25-84) and copy them onto the chart. Copy in the number of repetitions from Level 1.

To help you in this task, I've included an example of my Workout Prescription on page 23.

Now that you have written your Body Part Specific prescription for today, go for it!

I suggest a program of three days a week for one week. At the end of each exercise session, evaluate subjectively how you are doing. If the exercises seem to be too much for you, cut the number of repetitions in half (this includes the repetitions for the Warm-Up and Cool-Down exercises as well) until you are able to do them comfortably. (If you are already doing Warm-Up and Cool-Down exercises in your ongoing fitness program, and you have mastered them, don't cut them in half when using them with your Body Part Workouts.) When you can do the body part exercises comfortably, increase the prescribed number of repetitions on one of your three days in the week. When that becomes comfortable, increase it to two days a week, etc. When you get to the point where you can do the entire sequence three days a week comfortably, and you can continue doing it comfortably for three weeks straight, consider moving up to Level 2.

If you adapt quickly and after the first week have no difficulty adjusting to Level 1, move up to Level 2. If you experience difficulty doing Level 2 work, return to Level 1 while maintaining the Warm-Up and Cool-Down exercises. When this is comfortable for three weeks, increase the Body Part workouts to Level 2.

When you are comfortable with Level 2, introduce your next body part according to the chart that follows.

If at any time you feel exhausted or unusually overworked, drop one or both body parts one level until you are again able to do the exercise session comfortably three times a week for three weeks.

To simplify the foregoing, use the convenient chart that follows as a guideline. I recommend you stay at each new plateau for three weeks before moving on to the next (and more difficult) plateau.

If you are honestly pleased with the reaction of all four body parts, you might consider moving to Part III: A Total Body Program For Life. Before moving to Part III, however, you should have safely and comfortably reached Level 2 on all four of your priority body parts.

Weeks	Body Part 1	Body Part 2	Body Part 3	Body Part 4
1-3	Level 1			
4-6	Level 2			
7-9	Level 1	Level 1		
10-12	Level 2	Level 1		
13-15	Level 2	Level 2		
16-18	Level 1	Level 1	Level 1	
19-21	Level 2	Level 1	Level 1	
22-24	Level 2	Level 2	Level 1	
25-27	Level 2	Level 2	Level 2	
28-30	Level 1	Level 1	Level 1	Level 1
31-33	Level 2	Level 1	Level 1	Level 1
34-36	Level 2	Level 2	Level 1	Level 1
37-39	Level 2	Level 2	Level 2	Level 1
40-42	Level 2	Level 2	Level 2	Level 2

Progress Chart—All exercise programs should progress at a speed that gently but regularly increases effort as the body adapts to an increased workload. The exerciser should never overdo it, however. For the first three weeks, for example, concentrate only on one body part, and do the exercises at the Level 1 exertion. If, after three weeks, you feel you have mastered the exercises at Level 1, move them up to Level 2 for the next three weeks. If, however, you reach a point where the exercise level is too much, either stay at that level or drop back until the exercises become something you can handle before moving to the next level.

WORKOUT PRESCRIPTION FOR 1-4 BODY PARTS

DATE: 2/12/89

WARM-UP: page: **BODY PART:** Abdomen   page: 62-67

REPS	EXERCISES	REPS	EXERCISES
5/5	Knee + thigh Stretch	10/10	One-Legged Leg Curl to Chest
10	Sky Stretch	10	The Bicycle
10/10	Side-to-Side Stretch	15	Crunches (Half Sit-up)
10/10	Swimming Motion: Backstroke	10	The Jack Knife
10/10	Swimming Motion: Crawl		
5/5	Leg Lunges to the Front		
10	Heel Raises		
10/10	Windmill Stretch		

BODY PART: Upper Arms   page: 34-42   **BODY PART:** Hips, Thighs   page: 71-76

REPS	EXERCISES	REPS	EXERCISES
15	Arm Extensions, Bent	15	Leg Extensions
10	Rising to the Occasion	15	Leg Crosses
10	Reverse Push-up	15	Three-Quarter Squat
10/10	Arm Curls, Palms Up	15/15	Lunge Squat

BODY PART: Lower Back   page: 51-54   **COOL-DOWN**   page:

REPS	EXERCISES	REPS	EXERCISES
10/10	One Arm Dead Lift	20	Marching
10/10	Reverse Leg Lifts	20	Arm Crosses
15	Arch Up	5	Half Squats
10	Sit-up through Legs	5/5	Leg Lifts to Back
		10/10	Windmills
		4	Dynamic Breaths
		5	Rag Doll Stretch
		5/5	Hand Stretch

Your Prescription—To help you along using this workout chart, I've filled in mine for four body parts. The Warm-Up and Cool-Down exercises come from my *Dynastride!* book, but you can use any set you find serves to loosen your muscles. The numbers with a slash mark (10/10) under the reps column merely refers to doing 10 repetitions per side. For instance, the Knee & Thigh Stretch should be done 10 times on each leg.

WORKOUT PRESCRIPTION FOR 1-4 BODY PARTS

DATE: __/__/__

WARM-UP: _____ page: _____

REPS	EXERCISES

BODY PART: _____ page: _____

REPS	EXERCISES

BODY PART: _____ page: _____

REPS	EXERCISES

BODY PART: _____ page: _____

REPS	EXERCISES

BODY PART: _____ page: _____

REPS	EXERCISES

COOL-DOWN _____ page: _____

REPS	EXERCISES

THE MIND

Success in everything we do in life can be traced back to one common factor: proper mental attitude. From being a good parent to winning an Olympic gold medal, the mind plays the most significant role. Think of the mind as an unexplored frontier; there is so much to be learned about how it works and so much to be explored regarding its tremendous potential. As in every other aspect of life, a successful fitness and exercise program begins and ends with the mind. If you don't mentally decide that you want to improve yourself, you won't! Many people resist change. But once they decide on that change, things get done. Make up your mind to change your body. It will change your life.

In Sync With Your Body—There is no physical human accomplishment possible without the full cooperation of the mind. The body can accomplish what the mind can conceive. Take time each day to build, in your mind, the body you want to inhabit for the rest of your life. And then take positive steps to follow through on that mental concept of the ideal you.

Level 1	1 minute
Level 2	3 minutes

THE SCALP

Few people think in terms of exercising their scalp. Although the process of shampooing the hair serves as a form of self-massage, there are some people, however, who go for scalp massages on a regular basis because they know the scalp is a very important element of good, healthy hair. It is also a factor in storing or relieving tension. For the regular exerciser, the scalp is especially important because during exercise, we lose about half of the heat that exercise generates through the head and scalp. Attention to good, healthy scalp is also very important for those who are in the habit of wearing hats, since hats tend to prevent the scalp from breathing properly.

Hair Pull—No, this is not a form of self-punishment. Spread your legs to shoulder width, bend your knees slightly, and bend forward, with your head lower than your heart. Now, pull your hair gently. This stimulates the scalp, and with your head lower than your heart, your body increases blood flow to the head and scalp.

Level 1	30 seconds
Level 2	1 minute

Scalp Massage—Give yourself a scalp massage with your fingertips. Don't be bashful. Do it vigorously. Really work that scalp as though you were kneading dough. This also serves as a good exercise for your fingers.

Level 1	30 seconds
Level 2	1 minute

THE EYES

Few of us exercise our eyes nearly enough. By reading this line of type, which causes your eyes to move from the left side of the page to the right, you are exercising your eyes much more than you are by watching television, where your eyes merely vegetate at the same spot. Rolling your eyes into the top of your head as an expression of exasperation is a form of eye exercise. We tend to forget that the eyes are serviced by an intricate series of muscles that form a latticework of opposing groups that are responsible for the extreme range of motion of the eye. The eyes need to be exercised as regularly as any other body part if we're to enjoy the full benefits of what they see.

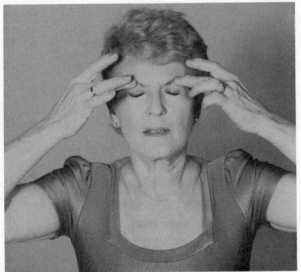

Eyebrow Flexes—Place your index fingers under your eyebrows just enough to apply gentle pressure and resistance. Now close your eyes tightly, applying pressure downward against the resistance of your fingers. Hold for a second and open your eyes.

Level 1	8 times
Level 2	15 times

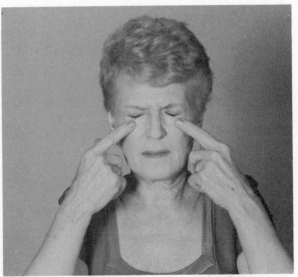

Lower Eye Flexes—Place your index fingers underneath your eyes just enough to apply gentle downward pressure and resistance. Slowly close your eyes as tightly as possible. Hold for a count of 3, then open them.

Level 1	8 times
Level 2	15 times

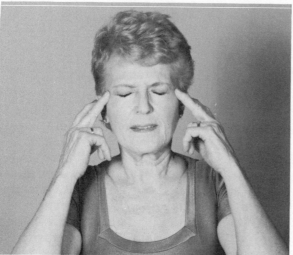

Side Eye Flexes—Place your index fingers just to the outside edge of your eyes; apply gentle pressure toward the outside of your head. Slowly close your eyes as tightly as possible. Hold for a count of 3, then open them.

Level 1	8 times
Level 2	15 times

Upward Outlook—Keep your head straight; do not lift your head. From this position, moving your eyes only, attempt to look at the ceiling above your head. Now, without pausing, bring your eyes downward, and once again, without moving your head, look at the floor.

Level 1	8 times
Level 2	15 times

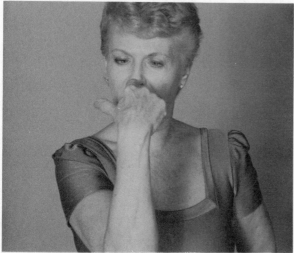

Bee On The Nose—Keep your head still and straight. Extend your right arm out straight in front of you. Extend the index finger. Now, very slowly, bring the index finger toward your nose, keeping your eyes on the tip of the index finger the whole time until your finger touches the tip of your nose. Now slowly move the index finger away from your nose, following it with your eyes.

Level 1	8 times
Level 2	15 times

Eyes In The Sides Of The Head—Raise both index fingers and hold them straight up in the air at the sides of your head about a foot from each ear. Now, without moving the head, attempt to look at first the right finger, and then rapidly shift to the left finger.

Level 1	8 times ea. way
Level 2	15 times ea. way

MOUTH AND CHIN

There are 55 muscles in the face. With these muscles, you smile, frown, laugh, weep, or show any other inner feelings through your facial expressions. Facial muscles must be used regularly to maintain tone and firmness. These muscles are subjected to the same laws of exercise as any other muscles in the body. As we age, the cheeks and jowls tend to sag from lack of use. Chewing our food is only one form of exercise and many commercially packaged or frozen foods today require only "soft" chewing. This alone is reason to exercise the facial muscles: without exercise, these inactive muscles will soon become less firm, especially around the mouth and chin.

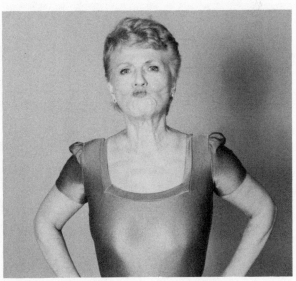

The Big Mouth—Open your mouth as wide as it will possibly go. Hold for a second, and then close your mouth, pursing your lips as much as possible, making a conscious effort to keep the muscles in and around the mouth tense at all times.

Level 1	8 times
Level 2	15 times

The Puffer—Keeping your mouth tightly closed, suck in your cheeks as far as possible, then immediately puff up the cheeks as much as possible. Repeat this exercise at a fairly fast clip.

Level 1	8 times
Level 2	15 times

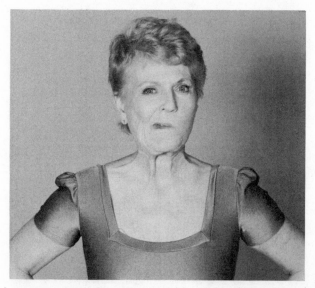 

Mobile Mouth—Purse the lips and twist your mouth as far as possible to the right, then immediately twist your mouth to the left as far as possible, keeping your lips pursed the entire time. Do this exercise smoothly.

Level 1	8 in ea. direction
Level 2	15 in ea. direction

The Thinker Speaks—Place your clenched fist under your chin just like the Rodin statue of "The Thinker," exerting gentle upward pressure. Without moving your head, open your mouth as wide as possible. Keep steady resistance on the chin without moving the head throughout the entire movement.

Level 1	8 times
Level 2	15 times

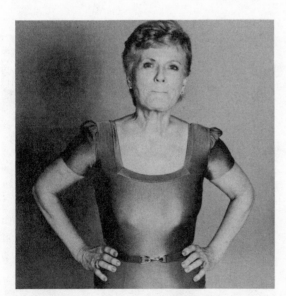 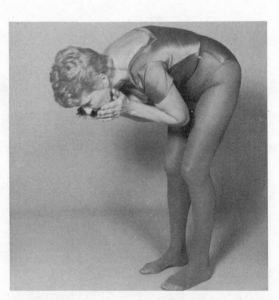

Lose Your Lips—Purse your lips and attempt to roll them into the inside of your mouth until you seem to have no lips left. Hold for a count of 3 and allow them to return to normal before repeating the exercise.

Level 1	8 times
Level 2	15 times

Face Pat—Bend over at the waist. Pretend that you are leaning over your bathroom sink, splashing water on your face. Instead of splashing water, however, gently pat your face for 10 seconds. Pause 5 seconds and repeat.

Level 1	8 times
Level 2	15 times

NECK AND THROAT

We often forget about doing exercises for the neck and throat. Therefore, as we age, the muscles in the neck atrophy from lack of use and we get what some people refer to as "turkey neck." It is especially noticeable when the head is bowed forward. To cover up this problem, many people wear clothes with high necklines. But, as with other areas of the body involving muscle groups, selected exercises done on a regular basis can help improve this condition.

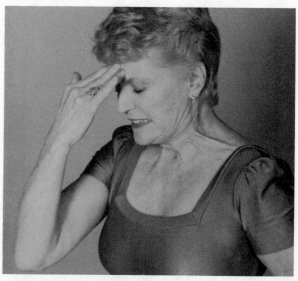

Up-And-Down Neck Conditioner—Place your fingertips on your forehead and apply gentle, constant resistance against your forehead. Lift your head up and look at the ceiling, then bring your head down, attempting to place your chin on your chest. Pause for a second and then bring your head back up to look at the ceiling.

Level 1	8 times
Level 2	15 times

The Thinker Speaks—Place your clenched fist under your chin just like the Rodin statue "The Thinker," exerting gentle upward pressure. Without moving your head, open your mouth as wide as possible. Keep steady resistance on the chin throughout the exercise.

Level 1	8 times
Level 2	15 times

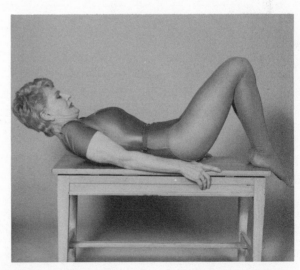

Head Raises—Lying on a bed or a bench, extend your head over the edge. Allow your head to loll back in a relaxed way, but just your chin out as far as possible. Now, while keeping your arms straight at your sides to help provide balance, raise your head as far as possible, trying to touch your chin to your chest. Hold for a second and return to your starting position.

Level 1	8 times
Level 2	15 times

Neck & Throat

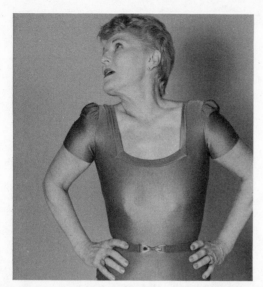

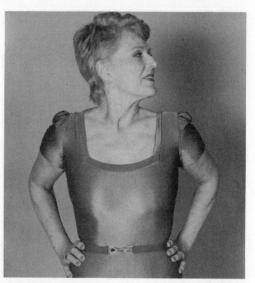

Neck Roll—Stand up straight with your legs a foot apart, your hands on your hips, and your shoulders squared. Allow your head to drop forward toward your chest until your chin hits your chest. Now, staying as relaxed as possible, roll your head to the right, following through by rolling it to the back and bringing it around on the left. Now reverse the direction.

Level 1	4 times
Level 2	8 times

Side-To-Side Neck Turns—Stand up straight, feet a foot apart, hands on hips, shoulders squared, head straight ahead. Now, keeping your head up straight, turn it as far as it will comfortably go to the right, then across to the left, then back to the right.

Level 1	8 times
Level 2	16 times

SHOULDERS

Too many people—both men and women—tend to go through life with poor posture, which is magnified later in life if some exercise is not done to counteract it. Good posture makes for better health, because it frees up the chest to do what it was meant to do: to serve as a compartment for the lungs, allowing the lungs maximum expansion, and therefore, maximum oxygen intake. Strong and flexible shoulders contribute to good posture. Good posture expands your chest cavity by bringing your shoulders back, which helps tighten your abdominal muscles. A few simple exercises for the shoulders, combined with good posture, will offer a multitude of benefits both inside and out.

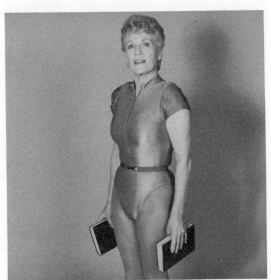

Lateral Arm Raises to Sides—Stand straight and tall with small books in hands. Keeping your arms straight the entire time, raise your arms laterally until they touch above your head. Slowly lower them back to the original position. (For Level 1, do the exercise without the books. As you improve throughout Level 2, increase the size and weight of the books.)

Level 1	8 times
Level 2	15 times

Arm Raises To Front—Stand straight and tall with small books in hands in front of thighs. Keeping your arms straight the entire time, slowly raise your arms out in front of you, ultimately reaching them straight above your head. Slowly lower them back to the original position. (For Level 1, do the exercise without the books. As you improve throughout Level 2, increase the size and weight of the books.)

Level 1	8 times
Level 2	15 times

Military Press—Stand straight and remember to keep that waist in. Start off by holding your cans or books out beside your ears. Now press your arms up overhead, pause, and bring them back down. (As you improve, increase the size and weight of the cans or books.) Using books or cans for weight provides resistance and offers greater effectiveness.

Level 1	8 times
Level 2	15 times

The Taut Towel—Using a common bath towel, grasp it firmly at both ends and pull it taut. Now, pull the towel to your side and upward with your right hand, while offering resistance with your left. When you ring it back down to your neutral position, pull with your left hand and offer resistance with your right. Repeat the process toward the left side of your body.

Level 1	4 in ea. direction
Level 2	8 in ea. direction

Parallel Towel—Holding a common bath towel at either end, pull it taut. Stand tall, waist in, arms at shoulder level. You are going to keep your towel parallel to the floor during this entire exercise. Pull the towel slowly to the left and resist with the right hand. Don't move the shoulders. Now pull the towel to your right and resist with your left hand. Repeat.

Level 1	4 in ea. direction
Level 2	10 in ea. direction

Shoulder Shrugs—Stand straight, feet shoulder-width apart. Relax your shoulders. Now, bring your shoulders up toward your ears, hold for a count of 3, then roll your shoulders back toward your back, holding for another count of 3, then return to the starting position.

Level 1	8 times
Level 2	15 times

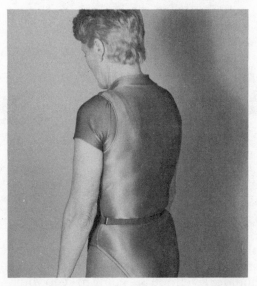 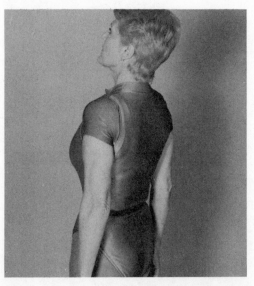

Walnut Walk—Begin in a relaxed position, your shoulders relaxed forward. Now, pretend that you're holding a walnut between your shoulder blades, and try to crack it. As the same time, try to crack an imaginary walnut between your seat. Notice how your posture improves and your stomach muscles become nice and tight. In this position, walk around the room. Relax and repeat it.

Level 1	5 times
Level 2	10 times

UPPER ARMS

One of the questions Jack and I get almost every time we do a lecture is, "What can I do for my sagging upper arms?" This is a common problem, especially in regards the back of the arm (tricep muscles). The tricep muscle is the muscle that extends the arm against resistance. Unfortunately, it does not get used too much by the average person. Whenever you straighten the arm, you use the tricep muscle. When you bring your fist into your shoulder, you are flexing the front of the arm (the bicep muscle). In order to firm these muscles, you have to do specific exercises for them. You can rejoice, however, because these muscles respond very quickly to exercise.

Tricep Arm Extensions, Bent—(For back of arm.) At Level 1, you should do this exercise without using cans or books. At Level 2, begin with small, light cans or books and as you become stronger, increase the size and weight of the cans or books. Grasp your cans with palms down. Lean over, bending your arms as you keep them close to your sides, knees flexed, elbows high. Now, try to raise your cans straight up. Return to the lowered position. Repeat.

Level 1	8 times
Level 2	15 times

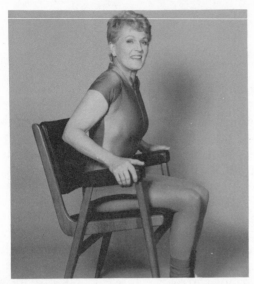

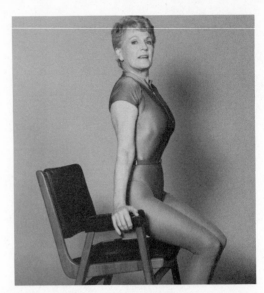

Rising To The Occasion—(For back of arm.) Sit in a chair with arms. Place your hands firmly on the arms of the chair. Now, lift your body out of the chair by using only your arms. You should feel the back of the arms doing most of the work.

Level 1	5 times
Level 2	10 times

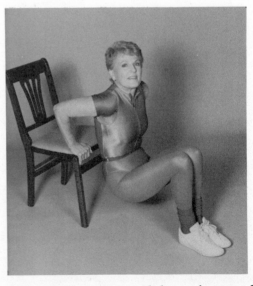

Reverse Push-Up—Sit on the edge of a sturdy chair. Make certain it is not going to slide out from under you when you use it. (You may want to rest the back of the chair against a wall.) Grasp the edge of the chair firmly with both hands. Gently slide off the edge of the chair and lower yourself toward the floor using your arms. Now, lift yourself back up to the edges of the chair.

Level 1	5 times
Level 2	10 times

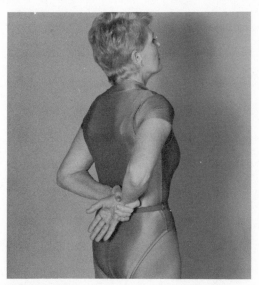 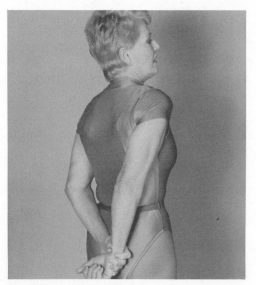

Wrist Wrestling—(For back of arms.) Grab your right wrist behind your back with your left hand. Pull up with your left hand as you resist by straightening your right arm. Reverse hands.

Level 1	5 times ea. side
Level 2	10 times ea. side

Arm Curls, Palms Up—(For front of arms.) Using a weight of some kind (books, canned goods, dumbbells, etc.), stand tall, waist in, with your arms extended in front of you, your elbows cocked. Hold your weights with your palms up. Smoothly but slowly lift the weights to your shoulders. Concentrate on the exercise. Return your arms to their original position.

Level 1	8 times
Level 2	15 times

Arm Curls, Palms Down—(For front of arms.) Using a weight of some kind (books, canned goods, dumbbells, etc.), stand tall, waist in, with your arms straight down in front of you. Hold your weights with your palms down. Smoothly but slowly lift the weights to your shoulders by bending your arms at the elbows. Concentrate on doing the exercise well, and on the muscles involved. Return your arms to their original position.

Level 1	8 times
Level 2	15 times

THE FOREARMS

The forearm is responsible for your ability to open and close your hand. This is accomplished by the interplay of the flexors and extensors, propinators and supinators. The forearms are involved in a great deal of everyday movement, especially movement of the hands and wrists, which include typing (I can feel the work the forearms are doing in holding my hands over the keys), working in the kitchen, and even operating a remote control device to change channels on the television. The forearms are also involved in any exercises that involve the upper arms, so the forearms are contributing in any action taken by the hands, wrists or arms.

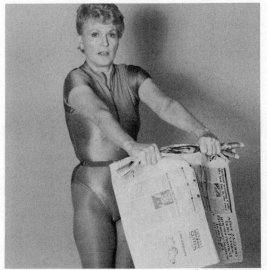

Newspaper Roll—Get a section of the newspaper and grasp an end of it in both hands. Extend your arms straight out in front of you and then begin to roll up the newspaper. Roll with a great deal of energy and speed. The more resistance you can make the newspaper provide, the better.

Level 1	8 times
Level 2	15 times

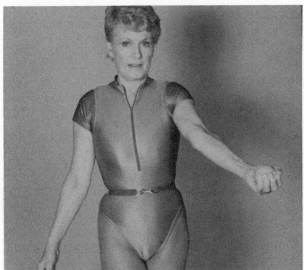

The Big Squeeze—Take a rubber ball that fits easily into your palm. Squeeze the ball as tightly as you can, hold for a count of 3, and then release. Repeat. (Get into the habit of carrying your ball with you. This exercise can be done just about anywhere at any time.)

Level 1	8 times
Level 2	15 times

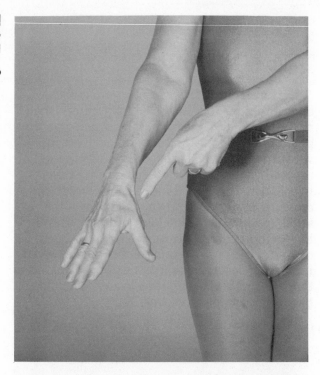

THE WRISTS

The wrist is the body part that joins the forearm and the hand. It works in conjunction with both and serves as a conduit of muscle impulses from the forearm to the hand while also serving as the joint on which the hand pivots. Most concern with the wrists come from two very opposite directions. People with thick wrists generally want smaller, more delicate wrists, and people with delicate wrists frequently want more strength in their wrists. As far as the size of the bones in the wrists go, there is little that can—or should—be done. Certain exercises, however, *can* make the wrists leaner, and similar exercises can make delicate wrists stronger by building up adjoining and underlying muscle tissue.

Wrist Flexes, Palms Down—Using two typical kitchen cans, extend your arms forward and hold the cans in each hand, palms down. Now, without moving your arms, raise and lower the cans using only your wrists. Do this exercise smoothly.

Level 1	10 times
Level 2	20 times

Wrist Flexes, Palms Up—Using two typical kitchen cans, extend your arms forward and hold the cans in each hand, palms up. Now, without moving your arms, raise and lower the cans using only your wrists. Make smooth movements.

Level 1	10 times
Level 2	20 times

THE HANDS

The human hand works in conjunction with the forearm and is one of the most marvelous devices in the world. The mobility of the human hand, its incredible dexterity, combined with the prehensile thumb, has made possible everything from tool-making to art, beautiful piano concertos and handshakes. The mechanism of the human hand is an intricate system of joints and pulleys, all controlled by impulses sent back and forth along nerves that stimulate individual—and often minute—muscles. The length of the bones in our fingers are predetermined, and little can be done to lengthen them. However, there is much we can do to strengthen the muscles in our hands, and much we can do to maintain dexterity.

Hand Flexes—Extend your hands out in front of you, palms up, ringers splayed. Now, very quickly, clench your hands into fist, and then quickly return them to the starting position in which you extend the fingers. This may look and seem relatively easy, but you'll notice that your hands become tired, especially if you are doing the exercise quickly. You can also do this exercise palms down.

Level 1	10 times
Level 2	20 times

 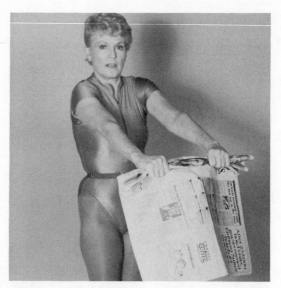

Shake-A-Hand—This one may seem extremely simple, but it isn't really. It should be done following the Hand Flexes—immediately after them. Hold your hands out in front of you and shake your hands. While shaking them, move your arms about in all conceivable positions.

Level 1	1 minute
Level 2	2 minutes

Newspaper Roll—Get a section of the newspaper, and roll it up. Do it with real force. Put some strength and determination into it. After you've rolled the paper up, unroll it. This one helps strengthen the hands and makes them more flexible.

Level 1	8 times
Level 2	15 times

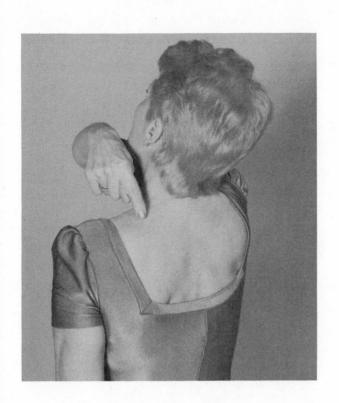

UPPER BACK

Many people over 50 have what can charitably be described as poor posture. This can be due to a variety of causes: congenital bone formation problems, poor posture in the formative years, an automobile or other accident affecting the back, or diseases associated with aging (such as kyphosis). Almost everyone can improve their posture, barring structural difficulties, by working on strengthening the upper back. When the muscles in the shoulders become weak, they tend to go forward; the muscles in the front become foreshortened and the muscles in the back become stretched out, causing bad posture.

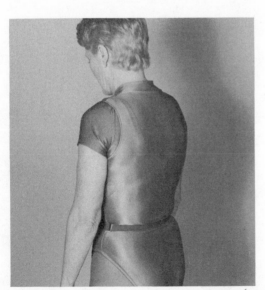

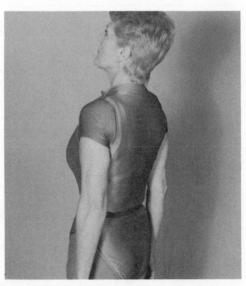

Walnut Walk—Stand up straight. Pretend that you are holding a walnut between your shoulder blades, and try to crack it. At the same time, try to crack an imaginary walnut between your seat. Notice how your posture improves and your stomach muscles become nice and tight. In this position, walk around the room.

Level 1	5 times
Level 2	10 times

The Towel Exercise—Stand as tall as you can, waist in, head up. Raise your towel overhead. Don't let your head go forward. Try not to move your body from side to side, just your arms. Pull down with the right arm, resist with the left arm, then reverse. Try to break the towel in two.

Level 1	5 on ea. side
Level 2	10 on ea. side

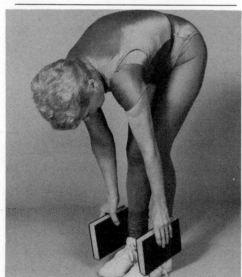

Rows, Bent At Waist, Arms In—Bend over with books close to the floor, knees flexed. Be sure to keep your head either parallel with the floor or hold it up. From this position, pull your arms up and to the back, keeping your arms close against your sides. Try to squeeze your shoulder blades together. Keep your elbows high. Pretend those books weigh 100 pounds each. Return to starting position.

Level 1	8 times
Level 2	15 times

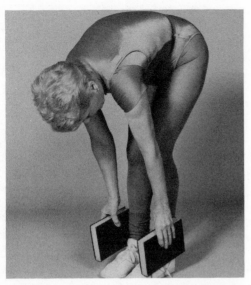

Rows, Bent At Waist, Arms Out—Bend over with books close to the floor. Be sure to keep your head either parallel with the floor or hold it up. From this position, extend your elbows out away from your body, then pull your arms up and to the back. Keep your elbows high. Pretend that the books are very heavy weights. Return to starting position.

Level 1	8 times
Level 2	15 times

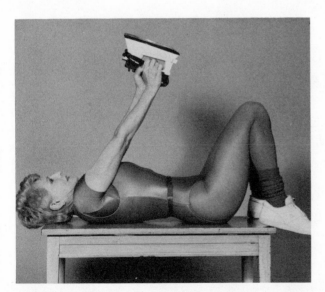
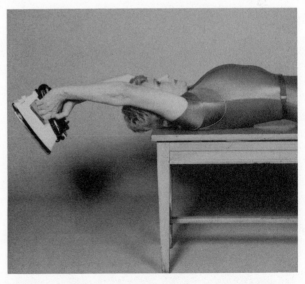

Pullover—Lie on the edge of a bed or bench, knees bent, heels near buttocks. Using a book or an iron or something else that will provide weight, extend the weight (held in both hands) straight up toward the ceiling. Keeping your arms straight, lower the weight down behind your head, pause, and slowly raise the weight until it is once again perpendicular to the floor. Start with a smaller weight and work up as you become stronger. Do this exercise smoothly.

Level 1	8 times
Level 2	15 times

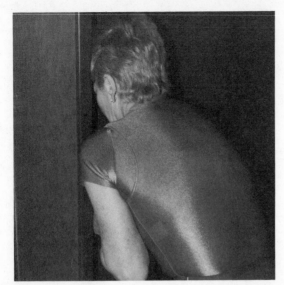 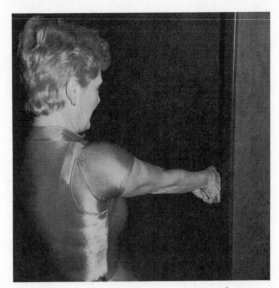

Door Knob Pull—Using a door knob that is very securely fastened, and pulling from the side of the door that opens outwards away from you, grasp the door knob in both hands, plant your feet close to the door, bend your knees, and lean back slowly, straightening your arms as you go. Once you've extended your arms to their limit, slowly pull yourself back to the door knob.

Level 1	8 times
Level 2	15 times

LOWER BACK

Practically everyone has had or will have a lower back problem at some time in their lives. There is probably no other portion of the human body that is so prone to injury and pain as the lower back. These problems can be caused by sitting too much, standing too much, and exercising too little. Often you will find a person with a weak abdomen also suffers lower back problems. Because every muscle group in the body has an opposing muscle group that works against it, many times it is a weakness in the opposing group that causes the problem. If you are considering a lower back exercise program, it would be worth your while to also consider taking up an exercise program for the lower back's opposing muscles.

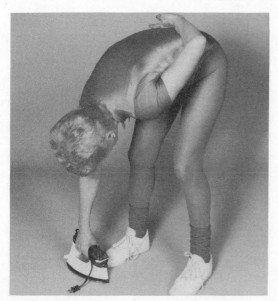

One Arm Dead Lift—Using a small weight (such as a clothes iron), set it on the floor. Now, bend at the waist and bend the knees slightly. Place your left hand behind your back. With the right hand, bend down and pick up the weight, straighten up and lean back slightly. Do the same thing using the opposite hand. As you progress to Level 2, you can consider using heavier weights.

Level 1	5 times ea. side
Level 2	10 times ea. side

Lower Back

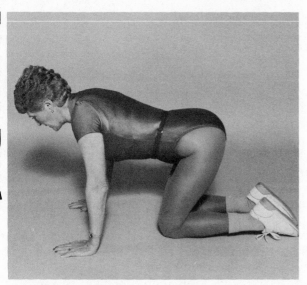 

Lower Back Hunch—On all fours, lift your chin and arch your back as much as possible in a smooth motion (without forcing it). Now try to put your chin on your chest and raise your shoulders to your ears, hunching your back. Repeat.

Level 1	8 times ea. way
Level 2	16 times ea. way

 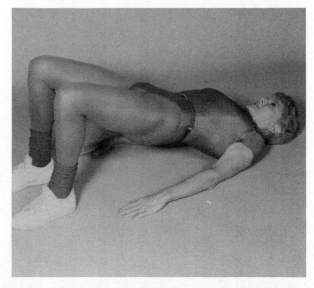

Arch Up—Lie on your back, knees bent, hands straight at sides. Now, lift your hips up off the floor to the point where you form a straight line from your knees to your shoulders. Lower yourself and repeat.

Level 1	8 times
Level 2	15 times

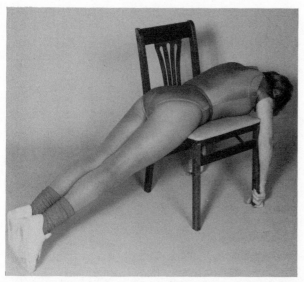

Reverse Leg Raises—Lie face down across a sturdy chair, with your head dropping forward. Grasp the legs in front of you with your two hands. Now, raise your head and lift boh legs at the same time, as high as you can. Try to keep your legs straight. Hold for a count of 1 and then lower yourself to repeat.

Level 1	8 times
Level 2	15 times

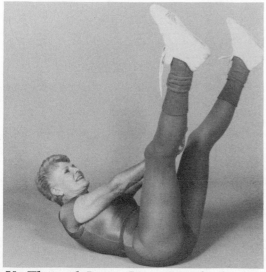

Sit-Up Through Legs—Lie on your back, arms and legs up in the air. Tuck your chin on your chest and sit up to your feet. Keep the legs in the air. Sit up and lie back again. Sit up, lie back. Keep breathing smoothly. Exhale through the mouth as you come up, inhale through the nose as you go back.

Level 1	5 times
Level 2	10 times

Lower Back Stretch—Lie flat on the floor or bed and grasp the back of right thigh and try to bring your knee into your chest. Keep back flat. Alternate with other leg. Variation: Grasp the back of both thighs and try to bring both legs into chest.

Level 1	Hold for 30 seconds
Level 2	Hold for 1 minute

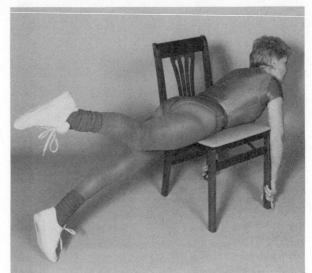

Leg Crossovers—Lie face down across a chair, legs spread apart, head up. Try to cross your legs. Left, right, left, right, left. Think into the thigh muscles. Make them work. Don't just flop your legs back and forth.

Level 1	8 in ea. direction
Level 2	15 in ea. direction

Alternate Leg Lifts, Face Down—Lie face down across a chair, chest supporting your body. Straighten your arms. Now, with your legs straight, lift right leg as high as you can, then alternate with left leg. Elevate head slightly as you lift.

Level 1	8 times ea. leg
Level 2	16 times ea. leg

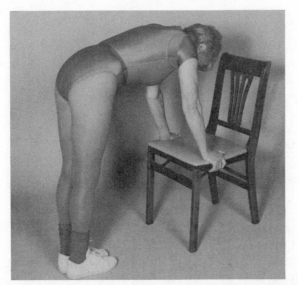

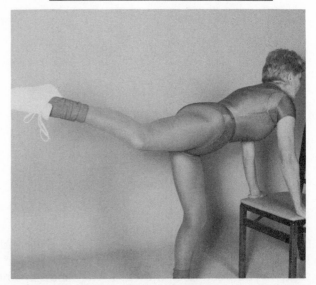

Alternate Leg Lifts, Bent At Waist—Bending at the waist, grasp both sides of a chair that is not going to slip when you put weight on it. Keep your back flat. Now, lift the right leg, pointing the toe. At the same time, lift your head. Hold for a second, and return to the original position. Alternate legs.

Level 1	4 times ea. leg
Level 2	10 times ea. leg

Chest

THE CHEST

So much emphasis is placed on the chest today. Women want a nice-looking bust, and men want a handsome, muscular-looking chest. These areas can be improved through exercise. The muscles that support the breast area—the pectoralis major and minor—help fight gravity and keep the breast area from hanging and sagging just as though you had an extra pair of hands to support them. Chest exercises generally involve themselves with *expanding* the chest, flexing the muscles around the ribcage, and strengthening the diaphragm. Besides the obvious benefits of looking better, there are a multitude of benefits these exercises bestow on the individual's ability to breathe deeper and easier.

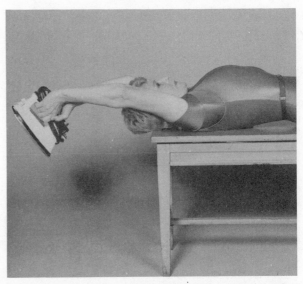

Pullover—Lie on the edge of a bed or bench. Using a book or an iron or something else that will provide weight, extend the weight (held in both hands) straight up toward the ceiling. Keeping your arms straight, lower the weight down behind your head, pause, and slowly raise the weight until it is once again perpendicular to the floor. Start with a smaller weight and work up in weight as you become stronger. Do this exercise smoothly.

Level 1	8 times
Level 2	15 times

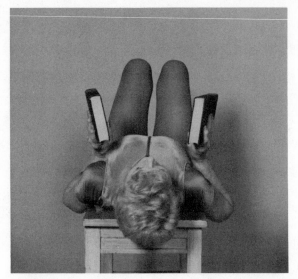

Arm Raises—While at Level 1, do this exercise without weights in your hands. As you become stronger, add books or cans as weights. Start with your arms curled at your sides while lying on your back on a bench or bed. Raise your arms as high as you can. Hold for a count of 3 and then bring your arms back to your sides.

Level 1	8 times
Level 2	15 times

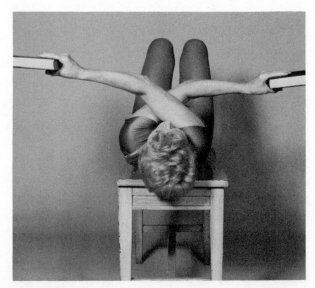

Arm Crossovers—Grasp a book in each hand (a paperback book at Level 1, a hardback at Level 2) and lie face up across a chair or a bench. Stretch your arms way out to the sides, then cross them over your chest and return them out to your sides.

Level 1	10 times
Level 2	20 times

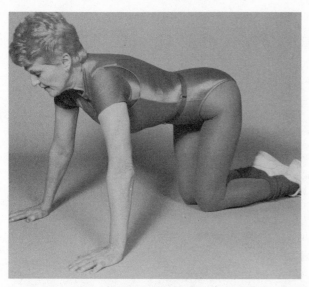 

Push-Up Number One—This is a relatively easy push-up for starters. Get down on the floor on your hands and knees. Now, lower your nose to the floor, touch the floor briefly, and raise yourself back up.

Level 1	8 times
Level 2	15 times

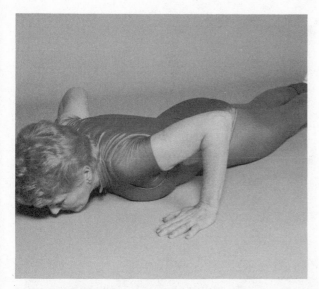 

Push-Up Number Two—This push-up is just slightly harder than the previous one. Lie on your stomach on the floor, hands out to your sides (hands under your shoulders), arms bent. Now push yourself into an upright position from the hips and thighs. Hold for a second, and lower yourself.

Level 1	8 times
Level 2	15 times

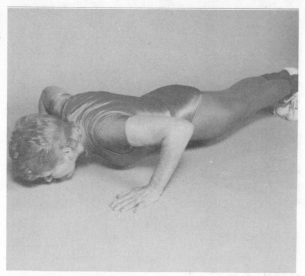 

Push-Up Number Three—This is the standard-issue push-up, the kind soldiers do. Lie on your stomach on the floor, hands out to your sides (hands under your shoulders), arms bent. Now, keeping your body ramrod straight, push yourself up so that you are supported only by your toes and your hands. Pause a moment and lower yourself.

Level 1	1-2 times
Level 2	5-10 times

 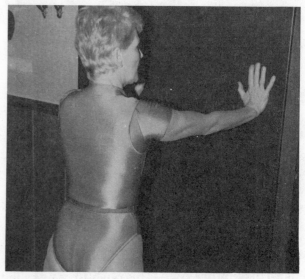

Push-Up Number Four—This is literally a vertical push-up. Stand in front of a wall, about two feet away from it, with your legs spread to shoulder width. Lean forward against the wall, and spread your hands against the wall. Now, push yourself away from the wall until your arms are straight. Pause a moment and lower yourself back toward the wall.

Level 1	10 times
Level 2	20 times

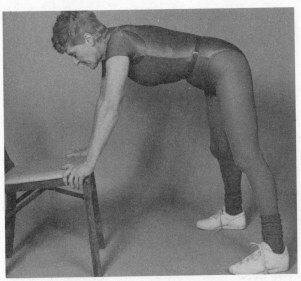

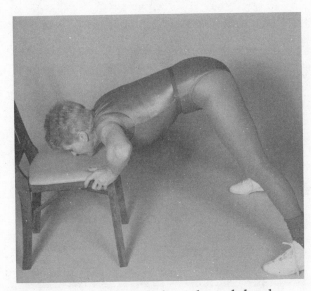

Push-Up Number Five—This is a relatively easy way to do a push-up. With your legs planted shoulder-width apart, bend at the waist and grasp the sides of a chair that is not likely to move while you put pressure on it. Now, keeping the 45-degree bend in your waist, and bending only at the ankles, lower your chin to the seat of the chair. Pause a moment, and push yourself back up.

Level 1	8 times
Level 2	15 times

Walk-Through—Extend your arms out to your sides at a doorway. Now, walk through the door, but keep your arms straight and grasp the doorway as your hands reach the frame. Push yourself forward against the resistance provided by your arms. Pause, back up, repeat.

Level 1	8 times
Level 2	15 times

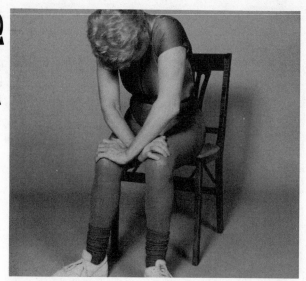

Inner Thigh Resistor—Sit down on a chair. Place your hands on the insides of the opposite knees. Now, while applying pressure against the knees with the hands, attempt to bring the knees together. Release just enough pressure to allow your knees to part, and then bring them back together, always applying pressure with the hands.

Level 1	8 times
Level 2	15 times

The Bustliner—Stand up straight. Now, clench your fists and bring them together at the wrists in front of your chest. You should also touch elbow to elbow. Now, press your elbows together as hard as you can for 5 seconds. Release. Press again, release.

Level 1	8 times
Level 2	15 times

60

Stick Exercise—You'll need a mop handle or a sturdy stick. Grasp the stick shoulder-width apart. Now, attempt to break the stick in the middle. Keep applying that pressure. As you are applying pressure, move your arms slowly across your chest to the left. Push with the right arm, resist with the left. Now, move your arms across your chest to the right, pushing with your left arm, resisting with the right. Don't move your shoulders, and keep the stick parallel to the floor.

Level 1	8 times
Level 2	15 times

THE ABDOMEN

One of the most neglected parts of the body is the abdomen. Although we frequently refer to the abdomen as the "stomach," it isn't really. The stomach is situated very high in the abdominal structure. Many refer to it as the "gut." The unfortunate thing about a weak abdomen is that it can have a very negative effect upon the small of the back (see Lower Back). A sagging gut is, of course, also unsightly. People frequently come up with interesting rationalizations as to why they have a sagging gut. In the end, however, it all comes down to one thing: inattention to developing and maintaining the abdominals. Fortunately there are a number of exercises for the abdominals, and, if done correctly, they work wonders!

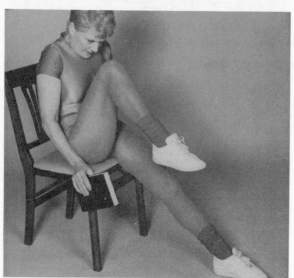

One-Legged Leg Curl To Chest—Sit on an armless chair. Grasp the side of the chair with your hands. Extend both feet out straight in front of you. Now, bring your right leg up to your chest, and then lower it. Repeat. When finished with the right side, do the same for the left.

Level 1	8 times ea. leg
Level 2	10 times ea. leg

Stomach Hunch—Try to put your chin on your chest and raise your shoulders to your ears. Round your back; tense your stomach muscles as you do this.

Level 1	8 times
Level 2	16 times

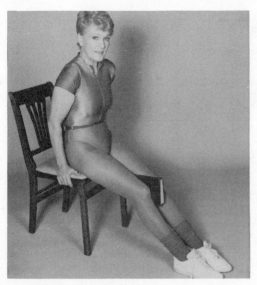

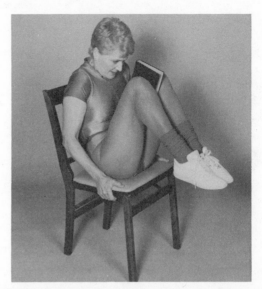

Double Leg Curl To Chest—Sit on an armless chair. Extend your legs out straight in front of you while grasping the sides of the chair with your hands. Now, bring your knees (together) to your chest, pause, and lower them to the floor again. When you reach Level 2, do the exercise with a book clasped between your knees. This is more advanced than the One-Leg Curl.

Level 1	8 times
Level 2	15 times

The Bicycle—Sit on an armless chair, grasp the sides with your hands, and raise your legs off the floor and pedal as though you were riding a bicycle. Attempt to keep the legs as high as possible. Pedal, pedal. Attempt to go for 20 seconds and then take a brief (10 seconds) breather, and repeat.

Level 1	5 times
Level 2	10 times

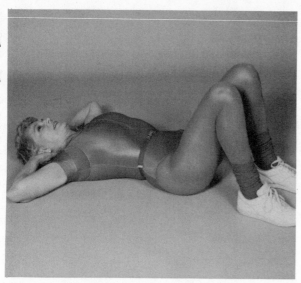 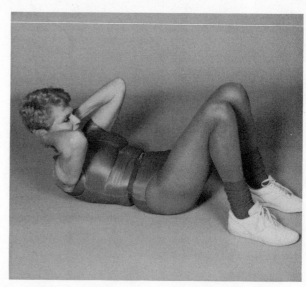

Crunches (Half Sit-Up)—Lying flat on your back, bend your knees, keeping your heels as close to your buttocks as possible, feet flat on the floor. Join your hands behind your head. Now, try to sit up to your knees. Exhale as you sit up; inhale as you lie down. Lie back down and repeat.

Level 1	8 times
Level 2	15 times

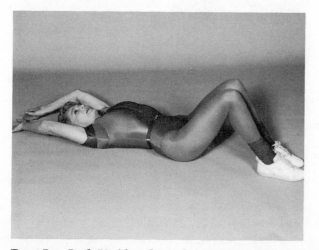 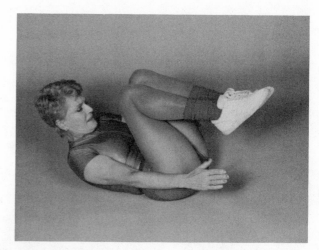

Bent Leg Jack Knife—Stretch out on your back on the floor, legs straight, arms overhead. Now curl your legs tightly into your chest. At the same time, raise your torso and try to touch your head to your knees. Stretch out again, come back up. This is an advanced exercise.

Level 1	8 times
Level 2	15 times

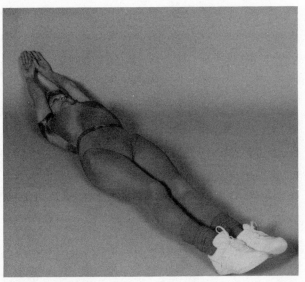

The Jack Knife—This is an advanced exercise for the midsection. Stretch out on your back on the floor, arms and legs rigid. Sit up and try to bring your legs up at the same time. Try to touch your toes. Return to the starting position.

Level 1	5 times
Level 2	10 times

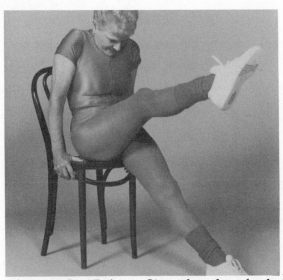

Alternate Leg Raises—Sit on the edge of a chair with both legs straight out in front, heels on floor. Keeping your left leg straight, lift it up as high as possible. Then lower it. Now do the same with the other leg.

Level 1	5 times ea. leg
Level 2	10 times ea. leg

Abdomen

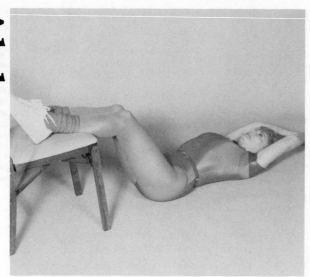 

Sit-Ups With Chair—Sitting on the floor, place your feet on a chair. Place your arms up above your head. Now, sit up and try to touch your toes. Lie back again, sit up, lie back, sit up.

Level 1	5 times
Level 2	10 times

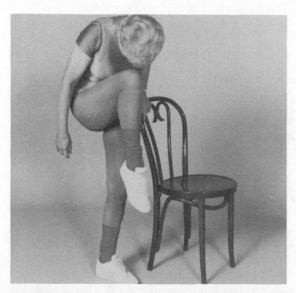 

Bent Knee Lift—Stand tall next to a chair that is placed against wall for support. Raise your left knee up as high as you can, trying to touch your forehead. Lower leg. Now do the same with the right leg.

Level 1	8 times ea. leg
Level 2	16 times ea. leg

Leg Circles—Sit on a chair, and grasp the sides of it with your hands. Point your toes and keep your legs together. Now, raising your legs off the floor, make circles with your legs together. Beginners should start with one leg and build to two. As you get better and better, make the circles larger and larger.

Level 1	10 circles
Level 2	20 circles

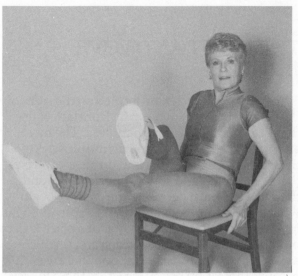

Leg Crosses—Sit down on a chair, grasping the sides with your hands. Spread your legs wide apart. Now cross your right leg over the left leg. Spread them wide again and cross the left leg over the right. Do 2 for each leg, then take a brief breather. Then do another set.

Level 1	8 times
Level 2	15 times

Leg Flutters—Sitting on the edge of a chair, with your hands grasping the sides, raise your legs off the floor and flutter your legs as though you were swimming. Continue doing this for at least 10 seconds each set for Level 1 and 20 seconds each set for Level 2.

Level 1	20 seconds
Level 2	40 seconds

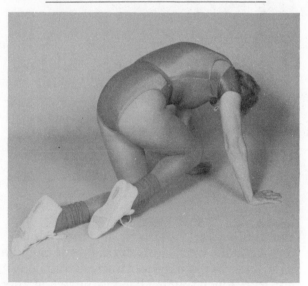

Bent Knee Into Chest—On your hands and knees, bring one leg forward into your chest, using short, rapid movements. When finished with the right leg, do the left.

Level 1	8 times ea. leg
Level 2	15 times ea. leg

67

THE WAIST AND LOVE HANDLES

The oblique muscles are located on the sides of the waist. When they collect fat from lack of use, they are often called "love handles." The most effective exercises for toning up the muscles of the waist involve twisting and turning: exercises that are simple—and simply effective. Beyond the age of 40, most people in the country begin what used to be called "middle-age spread." This involves excess body fat looking for a place to get out; the fat heads for the weakest areas, which are usually in the waist and abdominal areas, because there is no boney structure there to assist the muscles. Fortunately, a program of regular exercise can help.

Windmills—This is one of my favorites. Bend forward at the waist, arms stretched out. Simultaneously swing your right arm across your body and try to touch your left hand to the ceiling; then swing back your left arm and extend the right hand to the ceiling. Do this one rapidly.

Level 1	8 times
Level 2	15 times

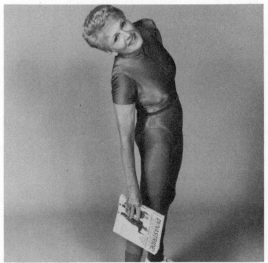

Sidebends With Book—A book or dumbbell provides added resistance to your exercise. This brings faster results. Start with the book in your left hand and press your right hand against the side of your head. Now bend to the left as far as you can. Try to touch your hand to the floor.

Level 1	8 times
Level 2	15 times

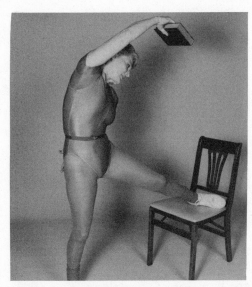

Sidebends With Chair—Place your left foot on a chair, but don't bend your leg. Now, with a book in your right hand, reach the book to the ceiling and lean to the left. Pause a moment and then bring the book down to try to touch the floor with the book in your right hand. Come back up quickly and repeat. Do the same movement for the opposite side.

Level 1	8 times
Level 2	15 times

Side Bends With Stick—Using a mop handle, place it behind your neck, grasping it firmly at either end. Exert some pressure toward the middle of the stick with both hands, and then begin doing bends from one side to the other. Begin with your arms bent, but as you improve, attempt the exercise with your arms straight. Try to do this in a smooth, effortless way.

Level 1	8 times ea. direction
Level 2	15 times ea. direction

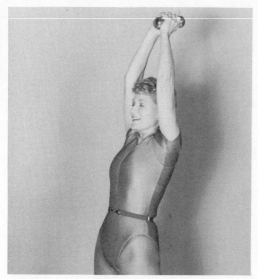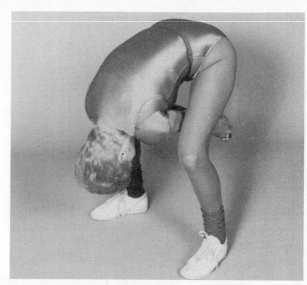

Dynamic Swings—For Level 1, do this without a weight. For Level 2, do this exercise with some sort of weight held in your hands. Stand with your feet shoulder-width apart; reach as high as possible overhead, stretching slightly to the back—swing smoothly down through your legs and back up again. Bend your knees slightly.

Level 1	8 times
Level 2	15 times

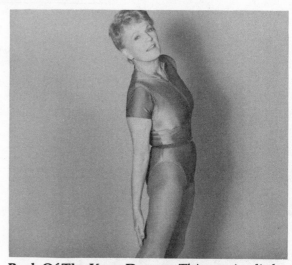

Back Of The Knee Dance—This one is a little difficult to show in a photo, because it moves fairly fast. Start by assuming the position I'm in in the photo. Extend the right leg, toe pointed (but touching the floor), and the right fingertips touching the back of the knee. Now, the object is to release from that position, and touch the left hand to the back of the left knee.

Level 1	8 times ea. side
Level 2	15 times ea. side

THE HIPS, THIGHS & BUTTOCKS

Hips, hips away. That's what we want to strive for. Again, fat will run to the spot where there's least resistance. Many of us sit too much. The more we sit, the more we cut off circulation. When we cut off circulation, the muscle becomes weak, fat collects around it, and the more the hips seem to expand. Especially for women, the hips are consistently a matter of concern. Under that fat, there are muscles pleading and yearning to be used. Regular exercise along with watching what you put in your mouth *does* deliver positive results in getting rid of unwanted body fat; and, a regular aerobic exercise program also helps burn away fat.

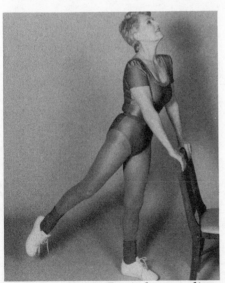

Leg Extensions—Begin by standing erect with your feet shoulder-width apart, your hands on the back of a chair that will remain stable. Now, point your toe, and then extend your right leg to the back as far as possible; then, move the leg out to the side as far as it will go; now, flex the foot (turn toes upward) and cross the same leg (right) over the opposite leg. Repeat on the other leg.

Level 1	8 times
Level 2	15 times

Alternate Leg Lifts, Face Down—Lie face down across a chair, chest supporting your body. Straighten your arms. Now, with your legs straight, lift right leg as high as you can, then alternate with left leg. Elevate head slightly as you lift.

Level 1	30 seconds
Level 2	90 seconds

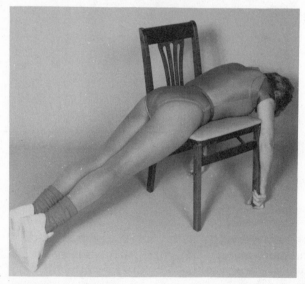

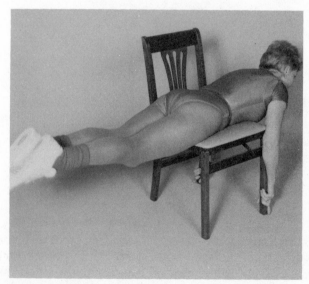

Reverse Leg Raises—Lie face down across a sturdy chair, with your head dropping forward. Grasp the legs in front of you with your two hands. Now, raise your head and lift both legs at the same time, as high as you can. Keep them rigid. Lower yourself to repeat. If you can't lift both legs, start with one, alternating legs.

Level 1	8 times
Level 2	15 times

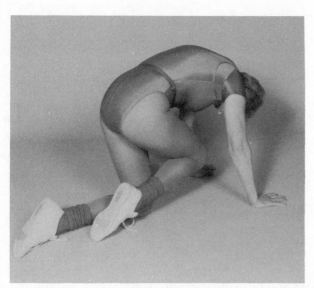

Donkey Kick—Although this is called a "kick," it is important to remember that you never kick, you lift your leg. On hands and knees, round back, head down, try to touch your knee to your nose. From this position, extend your leg to the back, keeping your back straight, looking at the floor in front of your fingertips. Repeat with opposite leg.

Level 1	8 times
Level 2	15 times

Leg Crosses—Sit down on a chair, grasping the sides with your hands. Spread your legs wide apart. Now cross your right leg over the left leg. Spread them wide again and cross the left leg over the right.

Level 1	8 times
Level 2	15 times

73

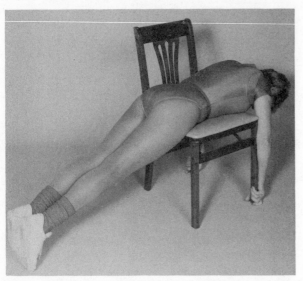 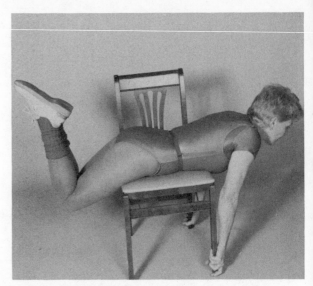

Hamstring Exercise On Chair—Lie down across a chair, grasping the legs with your hands, letting your toes touch the floor. Now, raise your head at the same time you curl your legs up together to attempt to touch your buttocks with the heels of your feet. Hold for a count of 3, and return to the beginning position.

Level 1	8 times
Level 2	15 times

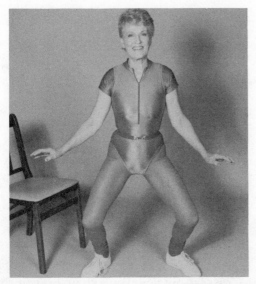 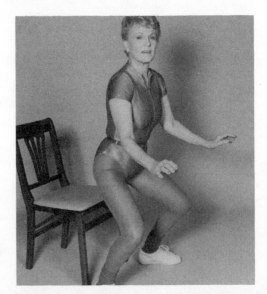

Three-Quarter Squat—These are effective for people who, because of knee problems, cannot safely do deep knee bends. Stand erect, feet shoulder-width apart; bend your knees, lean back slightly trying to keep your shoulders behind your heels.

Level 1	8 sets
Level 2	15 sets

Stand-Up—Sit in a chair. Now, hold your hands out in front of you both for balance and so that you can't use them to get up. Lift yourself several inches out of the chair without using your arms. Hold for a count of 3, and sit back down.

Level 1	8 times
Level 2	15 times

Leg Lunges To The Front—Stand erect, hands on hips (or on a chair for balance). Lunge forward similar to a fencing pose. Step back and lunge forward on the opposite leg.

Level 1	8 times
Level 2	15 times

Leg Lunges To The Side—Stand erect, hands on hips (or on a chair for balance). Lunge to the right with the right leg, step back and lunge to the left with the left leg.

Level 1	8 times
Level 2	15 times

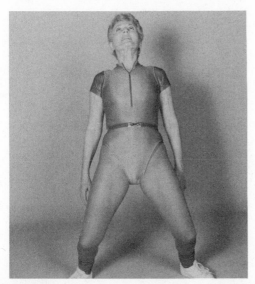

Sissy Squats—Because they are the easiest of all squats (and the easiest on the knees), these have come to be known as "sissy squats." Stand with your feet shoulder-width apart. Now, leaning back so that your shoulders are behind your heels, bend slightly at the knees. Hold for a count of 5.

Level 1	8 times
Level 2	15 times

Lunge Squat—This is a very good variation of the squat and the lunge. Balancing yourself on the back of a chair, step forward, lowering yourself several inches by bending your knees. Hold for a count of 5. Stand up straight again. Do it to the opposite leg.

Level 1	8 on ea. leg
Level 2	15 on ea. leg

Hips, Thighs & Buttocks

75

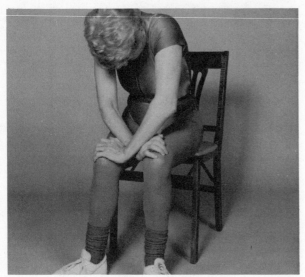 

Inner Thigh Resistor—Sit down on a chair. Place your hands on the insides of the opposite knees. Now, while applying pressure against the knees with the hands, attempt to bring the knees together. Release just enough pressure to allow your knees to part, and then bring them back together, always applying pressure with the hands.

Level 1	8 times
Level 2	15 times

THE KNEES

Your first response to a discussion of the knees might well be, "What in the world can be done to improve the knees?" Well, surprisingly enough, something can be done. Ideally, in a frontal view, the knee should be the narrowest point between the mid-thigh and the calf on the lower leg. On some people, the area in and around the knee is almost indistinguishable from the rest of the leg. In those instances, excess flesh around the knee detracts from rather than contributes to the overall effect of the leg. There are also several very good exercises that can be done indoors that will slim down the knee area, and assist the joint in functioning more easily and smoothly.

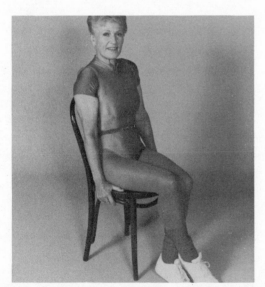
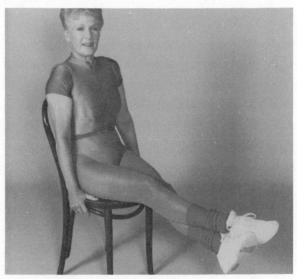

Self-Resisting Leg Extensions—Sit in a chair, feet on the floor. Cross your right ankle over your left ankle. Raise your legs slowly, and press down hard with your top leg against the bottom leg. Drop your legs to the floor and repeat again. Keep the waist in as you bring your legs up once more. Alternate.

Level 1	4 with ea. leg
Level 2	10 with ea.leg

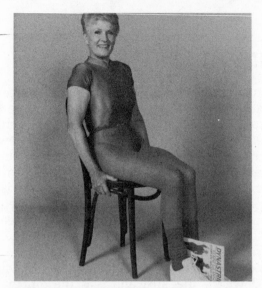 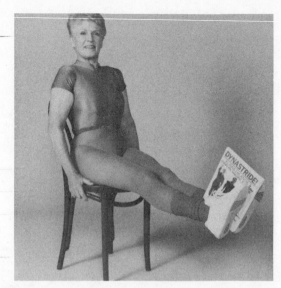

Leg Lifts With Book—Sit on a chair, your hands grasping the sides. Place a book between your ankles. Now, lift your legs up together, keeping the book firmly between your ankles. Hold out straight for a count of 5, then lower your legs. Repeat.

Level 1	8 times
Level 2	15 times

LOWER LEGS AND CALVES

The calf (the upper back of the lower leg, a.k.a. gastrocnemius) is the muscle group that has the most closely-bunched muscle fibers in the body. It is also the muscle that contributes greatly to the visual impression of a well-sculptured leg (in both men and women). In women, the calf is often exaggerated (sometimes to extremes) due to a tendency (at least in the past) to wear high heels. High heels are a fashion statement that has always undermined the human leg by encouraging short Achilles tendons (the tendon that joins the bottom of the calf with the heel of the foot). The lower leg workouts included here are a combination of exercises to strengthen and shape the lower leg, and stretches to condition and flex the Achilles tendon.

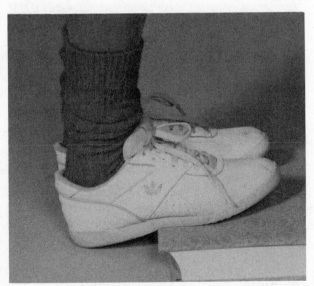

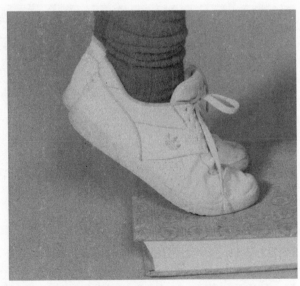

Toe Raises On Book—This exercise can be done either on a sturdy book or a block of wood. Holding onto a chair for balance, place your toes on the edge of the book or block of wood. Now, lower your heels to the floor, hold for a count of 2, then lift your heels up off the floor as high as you can, trying to stand on your toes for a count of 2.

Level 1	8 times
Level 2	15 times

Toe Raises: Toes Out—Using a chair for balance, stand with your feet about 18 inches apart. Turn your toes outward. Now, raise yourself on your toes. Hold for a count of 5, then lower yourself. Repeat.

Level 1	8 times
Level 2	15 times

Toe Raises: Toes In—Using a chair for balance, stand with your feet about 18 inches apart. Turn your toes inward. Now, raise yourself on your toes. Hold for a count of 5, then lower yourself. Repeat.

Level 1	8 times
Level 2	15 times

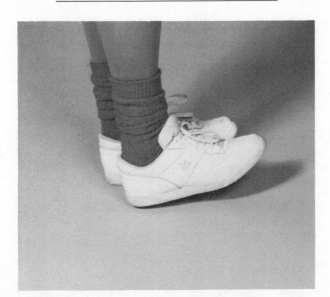

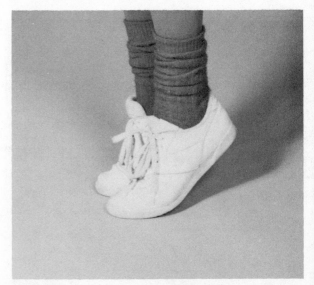

Heel Walk—This one takes a fairly good sense of balance, but with a little practice it becomes easy. Stand on your heels and walk 10 steps on each foot. Drop back to your soles. Repeat.

Level 1	8 times
Level 2	15 times

Toe Walk—Be careful to practice this one gradually, building up your sense of balance as you improve. Go up on your toes and walk around the room on your toes, taking 10 steps on each foot. Then drop back to your soles and take a short breather. Repeat.

Level 1	8 times
Level 2	15 times

ANKLES

As we discussed in regards to the wrists, the size of your bones has a great deal to do with the size of your ankles. But other aspects of the ankles can cause them to be shapely or shapeless. One of the factors, certainly, is body fat. An ankle that is not used tends to atrophy and build up fat. Additionally, people who spend their lives in jobs where they stand or sit a lot tend to exaggerate the ankles when tissue swelling associated with these positions sets in. Fortunately, the ankle is a highly flexible body part. Through a combination of exercises, flexibility routines, and getting into the habit of propping your feet up whenever possible, your ankles can be improved significantly.

Hopping—This one reverts to childhood, which is why it's so much fun. Hop on one foot for 8 times, then hop on the other foot 8 times. Keep alternating between feet.

Level 1	8 times ea. foot
Level 2	8 times ea. foot

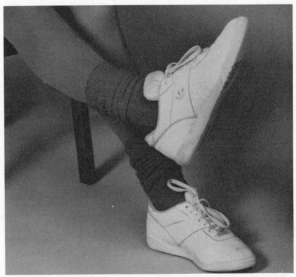

Ankle Circles—This one is extremely easy and very good for stiff ankles. Sit on a chair, and raise your right foot off the floor, straightening the leg. Now rotate your foot on your ankle, making circles as you do. Make 8 circles and then return your foot to the floor and do the same thing with the other foot.

Level 1	8 times ea. foot
Level 2	15 times ea. foot

Ankles

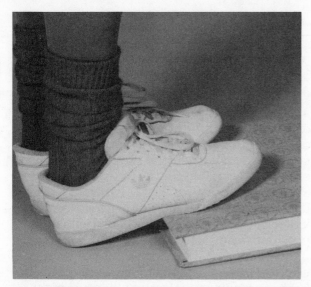 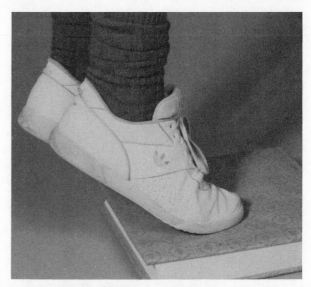

Toe Raises—Using a chair for balance, place a book or a slab of wood on the floor. Stand on the edge of the book or wood. Slowly lower your heels to the floor, pause, then slowly raise yourself up to your toes. Hold for a count of 3, then return to the neutral position. Repeat.

Level 1	8 times
Level 2	15 times

FEET

I don't believe that it takes a philosopher to make a statement like this: "When your feet hurt, you hurt all over." And I don't think we'd have to hire Mr. Gallup to take a poll to allow me to make this statement: "Well over half the people in the United States over the age of 50 suffer from some sort of foot problems." Often these problems are due to heels that are too high, shoes that are too short for the foot, or shoes with pointed toes. The human foot is a marvel of integrated bones doing a massive amount of work, but by pushing and shoving and forcing them into uncomfortable shoes, they become abused and yell for help. A program of good foot care will provide the help your feet are yelling for.

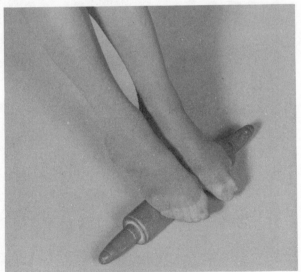

Rolling Pin Roll—This one is actually somewhat easier to do without socks or stockings. Roll your feet over the rolling pin that's on the floor; roll it back and forth, back and forth. This is an excellent one to do while you're watching TV at the end of the day.

Level 1	1 minute
Level 2	2 minutes

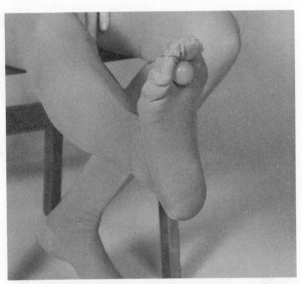

The Toe Grip—This one, also, is easier without stockings. Place a large marble or a small ball on the floor. Now, pick it up with your toes and raise your leg until it is parallel to the floor. Hold for a count of 5, drop the marble, and repeat.

Level 1	8 times
Level 2	15 times

Walking

THESE FEET WERE MADE FOR WALKING

What follows are some photos on fitness walking: what Jack and I call Dynastriding! As discussed in Part I of this book, the first body part you should get into shape is your heart. Without a strong, healthy heart, and an ambitious aerobic program at the heart of your overall fitness program, your efforts are very hollow. Vigorous walking is the easiest, most injury-free form of exercise you can take up. And besides serving as a basis for your fitness, it is also a terrific way of getting around. In Part III of this book I'll outline what I call "A Total Body Program For Life." One of the main ingredients of that program is a regular walking program.

Walking The Dog—I can't say enough good about the overall benefits of a regular walking program. There is nothing like an early-morning walk. It is invigorating and refreshing, and is excellent for the heart and lungs, and perfect for building up the hips, thighs, lower legs, knees, ankles, and feet.

Level 1	20 minutes
Level 2	40 minutes

Walking With Your Favorite Person—Don't overlook the opportunities to go on walks with friends and loved ones. I really enjoy taking walks near our home with my husband Jack. It provides for some special times away from the phone and from business, and it allows us to catch up on our day.

Level 1	20 minutes
Level 2	40 minutes

YOU'RE ONLY AS OLD AS YOU FEEL—Jack and Elaine, despite a vigorous schedule of travel for personal appearances, manage to fit their exercise regimen into every day's schedule. The results speak for themselves.

PART THREE

A Total Body Program For Life

Chapter 5

Gauging Pace

What should the dedicated exerciser expect from a solid, viable fitness program?

From the thousands of over-50 exercisers I've encountered over the last decade, there seems to be four primary benefits for which they strive:

1. Good health.
2. More energy, strength, flexibility.
3. A more youthful-looking body.
4. Elevated self-esteem.

What makes a successful exercise program?

1. A physical examination before beginning in order to assess current physical condition.
2. The exercise must have an aerobic base.
3. The exercise should work as many muscles as possible.
4. The exercise should stress the body in order to strengthen the body as it grows more used to the exercise.
5. The exercise must stop short of an intensity where it will cause injury or burnout.
6. The exercise must be performed regularly.
7. The exercise must be set up in a series of cycles so that it provides rest (recuperation) periods on a weekly, monthly, and yearly basis because a working muscle does not grow stronger if it is not provided with adequate rest and recuperation periods.

The primary focus of this book and the programs it contains is to improve specific body parts along with concentrating on an overall exercise program. You wouldn't take your car to a body shop to have the dents taken out and never lubricate the engine. The same with the body: it needs regular maintenance. That is why it is important to not only work on the specifics, but also on your overall cardiovascular fitness. Once you're satisfied with the improvement of your body parts, don't neglect them or you'll be right back where you started.

It is assumed, as stated in several other places in this book, that you have built a fitness base before putting more effort forth on a program of improving specific body parts. Your fitness base program, whether it is merely an adequate one or an ambitious one, is at the heart of any long-term improvement.

(If you have no base fitness at this point, but still want to take on this fitness program, be certain to faithfully do your Warm-Up and Cool-Down exercises in order to avoid the chance of injury.)

Now we want to join your base and your body specific goals and present an easy-to-follow program that will work for you year-round. We'll start with a weekly program and work into a monthly program, followed by a six-month schedule that combines aerobic workouts and specific body part workouts with periods of rest and recuperation.

When you feel ready for it, you can begin the six-month program simply by deciding on a date to start, and then making it your very own program for the next year.

The workouts are all geared toward your specific needs and ability levels, because the entire program is regulated by your pulse rate (see the next segment of this chapter). Therefore, the program will progress only as quickly and as far as is right for you. Because of this, the year-long program is a self-repeating program of two six-month-long segments. By that I mean that when you've completed it once, you begin the program again, and it will not be exactly the same as last time because since it is regulated by your individual pulse rate, your progress dictates how fast or slow the progress in the second and third and fourth six-month segments are made.

This effectively allows you to continue your program for the rest of your life. Now, let's take a look at that self-regulator, the pulse rate, and we'll review how it works.

HOW TO GAUGE YOUR EFFORT

Take a moment here and look ahead to the exercise programs. Note that the portions involving aerobic exercise (walking, running, cycling, swimming, etc.) are not designated with a distance you must go to get your exercise for that day. There are no instructions to "Walk a mile" or "Swim 400 yards." Everything of an aerobic nature is based upon time and effort. Effort is indicated by one of the following percentages: 60%, 70%, or 80%.

The percentages refer to what is called the Working Heart Rate (WHR).

WHR is the percentage of your Maximum Heart Rate (MHR) at which you are performing work that is causing the heart and circulatory system to exercise. It is the range where you are doing some good to your heart and blood vessels and for your lungs. Maximum Heart Rate, of course, is the theoretical fastest you'd expect your heart to beat at your age. The older one gets, the lower this number falls. At the other extreme of your MHR is your Resting Pulse Rate (RPR). This is the number of times per minute your heart beats when you are at rest.

What is a typical pulse rate? About 70 beats per minute. For the average, relatively healthy person, the pulse rate can fluctuate anywhere from 50 to 90. Anything significantly over 90 becomes suspect. Anything under 50 usually indicates that you're in very good physical condition. Highly trained marathoners, for example, often have a resting pulse rate in the 30s.

THE IMPORTANCE OF RESTING PULSE RATE (RPR)

Your Resting Pulse Rate is something with which you should be familiar.

It is a good indicator of your current state of health.

Therefore, it is a good idea to take your RPR first thing in the morning before getting out of bed. There are two reasons for doing this:

1. Charting your RPR over months and years will give you an indication of how your fitness program is progressing. As you become more fit, your RPR should fall. At some point it will stabilize, and you'll find that your body becomes almost like a clockwork mechanism. You'll be able to predict your RPR because it will always be within one or two points of where it was yesterday and the day before that.

2. The RPR serves as a barometer of your body. If your RPR has stabilized, and one morning you take it and it's elevated, you'll know something is not right. You may have contracted a cold or flu, stayed up too late, drank too much, or there may be some other reason for your RPR to be off. When it is high, you should explore possible reasons. If you are exercising faithfully, an elevated RPR is sometimes an indicator that your workout from the day before was more stressful than usual, and your body is not yet recovered. An elevated RPR due to exercise indicates that it would be advisable to cut back on the intensity and/or duration of your planned exercises for that day, giving your body another day to do the necessary repairs before stressing it further. A good exercise program should *never* have you scheduled for two difficult workouts on subsequent days. Your body needs time to recuperate from a hard workout before undertaking another one. Your elevated RPR may be just that: an indication that you worked hard yesterday, and that you should work easy or not at all today.

Taking the pulse rate is a very simple matter. You can take your pulse rate at either the neck or the wrist. The method you are likely to be most familiar with is at the wrist. The pulse in the wrist is located on the underside of the wrist, in the little hollow on the thumb side. Never take your pulse at the wrist by using the thumb of the opposite hand. Due to its size, the thumb has its own pulse and may interfere with picking up the wrist pulse. So, instead of grasping the wrist with the thumb, gently but firmly place your first and second fingers over the pulse point. When you feel it fairly clearly, count the pulse for 15 seconds and multiply it by four, or count it for 30 seconds and multiply by two. I prefer the latter method, because I feel if you are keeping daily track of your RPR you want the most accurate count possible. The *most* accurate method, of course, is to count for 60 seconds.

CALCULATING YOUR WORKING HEART RATE (WHR)

Working Heart Rate (WHR) is 60, 70, or 80% of your Maximum Heart Rate. It is the range where you are doing some good to your heart, lungs, and blood vessels. You'll need to know about your WHR in order to use the exercise programs that follow.

(For consistency, let me pick up the explanation I used in my book on walking, *Dynastride!*)

Somewhere between your Resting Pulse Rate (RPR) and your Maximum Heart Rate (MHR) is a range where your heart will begin to work harder because it is attempting to meet its bodily needs caused by exercise. It is in this range that your heart becomes stronger and your blood circulatory system is improved. This is also the point where exercise of an aerobic nature is helping the body thrive. Because of the gradual process of aging, this point is lower for a 50-year-old than it is for a 20-year-old. For the purposes of the programs that follow, we refer to this range as WHR—Working Heart Rate. The WHR range will be from 60 to 80 percent of your theoretical MHR (Maximum Heart Rate).

Here's how to go about determining your WHR (Working Heart Rate):

1. Start with the number 220.
2. Subtract your age (let's use 60). That gives us 160.
3. Now take percentages of the 160 that correspond to 60%, 70% and 80%. They come out to the following:

> 60% = 96 beats per minute
> 70% = 112 beats per minute
> 80% = 128 beats per minute

These are the three numbers you need to know to get the maximum benefits from the programs presented in this book. A gentle, starter's program would begin with workouts based upon 60%. Over a period of time, the exerciser would gradually work up to 70% and then ultimately 80%, but always using workouts at 60% as easy days or gentle workouts. As I mentioned before, aerobically speaking, we won't be concentrating on distance; we'll be working with time and effort (WHR).

The perfect opportunity to record your WHR is right now. Take a piece of scratch paper and figure out your WHR for 60%, 70%, and 80% of 220 minus your age and then write them on the lines in the box provided below:

My heart rate at 60% will be ____ beats per minute.
My heart rate at 70% will be ____ beats per minute.
My heart rate at 80% will be ____ beats per minute.

Remember these three numbers, because they will serve as your effort guides for the programs that follow. There is a place on each of the exercise pages for you to write in the three numbers so you don't have to keep turning back to this page.

Remember that without these numbers, your program won't work. They are numbers that will keep you from going too fast—and, just as importantly, they'll keep you from going too slow!

Chapter 6

The One-Week Trial Run

I have chosen a week as a trial run to see if you are ready for a long-term fitness regime that would become your way of life. A week is a good measure of time with which most of us are familiar and comfortable, so it serves as a mini-program which includes all the essential elements and theories used in the month and six-month programs. These elements are the hard/easy training concept, variety in exercising, and rest.

Hard/easy: The process used to improve the efficiency and power of a muscle is to stress it beyond its normal daily use, then to rest the muscle so it can recover, and then to stress it again, and rest it again. With each rest following stress, the muscle is able to do more work the next time it is exercised.

Because you do a relatively hard workout on Tuesday does not mean that you should take the next day off from exercise. Instead, the next day can be used for some easy exercising, or, even more importantly with the programs that follow, you can exercise some other part(s) of the body, thereby giving the part that was exercised hard on Tuesday an easy day on Wednesday.

Variety: In any exercise program, variety is all important. My husband Jack advises exercisers to completely change their program every two or three weeks. By this he means not only change the sequence of workouts, but change the type of

exercise and sport you are doing. I agree with Jack that incorporating such variety into your program keeps you from burning out and also prevents one set of muscles from becoming overworked. But I feel that much the same thing can be gained by putting together a program that is composed of exercising many different parts of the body in many different ways. A runner who does nothing but run will overwork certain muscles, underwork other muscles, set himself up for injury, and probably ultimately get bored and burned out.

The programs in this book, however, incorporate a variety of disciplines into a complete body workout. Those elements include: cardiovascular fitness (heart, lungs, and blood vessels) through aerobic workouts, workouts aimed at your problem zones (the prime concern of this book), Warm-Up exercises (including stretches to help prevent injuries and stiffness), Cool-Down exercises (to limber up the muscles after workouts so they are made ready for the next workout), and that most important element, rest.

Rest: Rest is the element that allows the stress you've put on your body and its muscles to convert into greater strength and endurance. It also revives the body so that the next time you exercise, you are able to do so more effectively because nature has restored your reserve.

A person cannot expect the human body to go and go and go endlessly without the proper amount of rest. Some people even abandon their entire exercise lifestyle because they fail to rest adequately and the exercise therefore seems to be too much for them to handle.

Rest is a combination of good, wholesome sleep at night, as much stress-free time as possible during the day, and regular attention to giving yourself some down time every day.

Something you will find as you get farther into a regular program of physical exercise is that a good, well-balanced program does promote deep, restful sleep at night. And there's nothing that can recharge the batteries like a good night's sleep.

THE ESSENTIAL PRIORITIES

There are two essential exercise components: cardiovascular fitness (the foundation of all good fitness and exercise) and body part improvement through repetition of exercises. So much has been said about aerobics and cardiovascular conditioning that it tends to become confusing.

Cardiovascular exercise is any aerobic exercise done regularly. In recent years the word aerobics has been used by aerobic dance studios and dance teachers to refer to *their* form of aerobic exercise. In actuality, the word *aerobics* has the broader meaning taught by my friend Dr. Kenneth Cooper of Dallas, Texas, who in 1968 wrote the landmark book *Aerobics*. In that book the word aerobics referred more commonly to jogging and running, since those were the most simple forms of exercise that Dr. Cooper recommended for gaining points on a weekly basis in order to fulfill the needs of the program.

Aerobic exercise (exercising non-stop for at least 12 minutes) includes (but is not limited to) the following exercise pursuits: jogging, running, aerobic dance, cross-country skiing, rope-jumping, swimming, sustained bicycle riding, running in place, working out on a mini-trampoline, circuit training, and Dynastriding. (Dynastriding is the exercise of walking at a tempo and speed that causes the Working Heart Rate to rise, while bringing the arms and legs very vigorously into the workout. The exercise is extensively covered in my book *Dynastride!*)

Aerobic exercise should be at the heart of *any* exercise program! All aerobic workouts are based upon time and effort and not upon distance.

When you examine the workouts in Part III of this book, you'll find that aerobic exercise is an essential part of the program. Regular aerobic exercise is a must if the program is to be of any benefit. That is why I have included Dynastriding four times a week. This gives you aerobic exercise on a regular basis to help build your strength and make the body part exercise easier.

The other priority, of course, is the basis of this book: reshaping specific body parts or your problem zones.

This is done primarily through repetitive use of that body part on a regular basis in an effort to slim it down and shape it up. There are two elements involved here. The first is to improve the parts of the body with which you're concerned, and the second is to maintain those body parts once you've got them in shape.

You've picked out your problem zones that need most attention. We'll work on those first, and as the program progresses and we add new body parts for work, we'll continue to maintain those on which you've worked so hard to improve.

Our ultimate goal will be to get all body parts into condition. And once you reach that point, it becomes a matter of maintaining them with a program that features an aerobic base, and a regular program of attention to all the muscles in your body. It sounds like a tall order, but it really isn't.

APPROACHING THE TEST WEEK

For the exerciser who is not a beginner and who has progressed through an aerobic fitness base and who has been regularly exercising the body parts selected in Chapter 4 of this book, the week that follows is not especially strenuous.

The week's worth of exercising is not meant as a beginner's week of exercise, however. It assumes a basic aerobic fitness and a modest familiarity with exercising the priority body parts. (If you are embarking on this program without a fitness base, disregard the aerobic portion. Be extra certain to do the Warm-Up and Cool-Down exercises, however.)

The week also gives you a taste of what is coming in the programs that follow: for a month, for six weeks, and for the rest of your life.

Begin this program next Sunday. You bought this book, you've read it to this point, you're enthusiastic, so let's go.

If you have not yet become comfortable with a

regular aerobic program and a regular body parts program, it is advisable to drop back and develop those skills before embarking on the program that follows. As stated before, however, if you wish to start without the benefit of an aerobic program, be certain to do a regime of Warm-Up and Cool-Down exercises before and after each exercise session.

If the week of exercise goes well, it is very likely that you are ready to schedule the month's worth of exercising into one of your upcoming months. (We'll also talk about that more after the week's exercising and in the first part of Chapter 7.)

THE ESSENTIAL PARTS OF THE EXERCISING GUIDE

If you are familiar with *Dynastride!* you'll recognize the basic exercise chart that follows. Except for a few changes, it is the same format.

I have done this for several reasons. The primary reason is that if you gained your aerobic fitness through the *Dynastride!* program, it is easier to work with a format with which you are already familiar. If you are not familiar with the *Dynastride!* program, but gained your level of aerobic fitness from some other source, I hope that you'll find the format I use here easy to follow and easier to use.

Let's take a quick review of the elements along the left side of the program before we begin:

Working Heart Rate: The box in the upper left is for you to note your WHR numbers as you figured them at the end of the previous chapter. These will come into play when doing aerobic workouts (see Total Scheduled Walking Time and Working Heart Rate below). Remember to recalculate these numbers each time you have a birthday.

Resting Pulse Rate: Measured at the wrist or the neck, the Resting Pulse Rate should be taken before getting out of bed each morning and recorded in the spaces provided. This should also be done on Rest Days when there is no exercising scheduled.

Warm-Up Exercises: This is in way of a reminder to do your Warm-Up Exercises before beginning that day's program.

Total Scheduled Walking Time: This is the total time of the aerobic side of the workout. I used Walking here because it is the simplest form of aerobic workout, and because those who have read and used *Dynastride!* will be familiar with it. Other methods of acquiring aerobic fitness may be substituted.

Working Heart Rate: The percentage of your Total Heart Rate for today's aerobic workout.

Body Parts: Simply fill in the body parts you have chosen as your priorities (see Chapter 4).

Cool-Down: As with the Warm-Up, a reminder for you to do your Cool-Down exercises following your workout.

Notes/Comments: This space is provided for you to jot down any observations you had on the day's workout. Did the aerobic workout today feel particularly easy? Did a sore calf muscle threaten to stiffen up again during today's Warm-Up exercises? By keeping some basic notes, you can review your reaction to workouts and by doing so adjust your future workouts to either take advantage of particular workouts that really helped you or to modify downward, particular exercises that caused you problems.

On days calling for aerobic *and* body part workouts, do the body parts directly after Warm-Ups and before the aerobic portion of the workout.

Regarding the body parts workouts, this week's workouts are based upon your doing a specific number of "sets" of the number of reps you are currently doing at Level 2 for that body part. Therefore, two blanks are on each body part line, i.e. 1. _____ × ____ sets. Fill in the body part on the first line, placing your current number one priority body part on line 1., your second priority on line 2., etc. You'll recall that your body part priority chart is on page 12.

In order to simplify the workout charts, I've screened out portions that are not applicable to that day.

Without further ado, let's move into your trial workout week:

My Working Pulse Rate
60% = 94 bpm
70% = 110 bpm
80% = 125 bpm

WEEK 1

	SUNDAY	MONDAY	TUESDAY	WEDNESDAY	THURSDAY	FRIDAY	SATURDAY
Resting Pulse Rate	80 bpm	72 bpm	76 bpm	76 bpm	72 bpm	72 bpm	72 bpm
Warm-Up Exercises	(X) Yes ( ) No	(X) Yes ( ) No	(X) Yes ( ) No	(X) Yes ( ) No	(X) Yes ( ) No	(X) Yes ( ) No	(X) Yes ( ) No
Total Scheduled Walking Time (Or Other Aerobic Workout)	Aerobic Workout REST DAY	Aerobic Workout	Aerobic Workout 40 min.	Aerobic Workout 20 min.	Aerobic Workout 20 min.	Aerobic Workout	Aerobic Workout 60 min.
Working Heart Rate	____% = ____bpm	____% = ____bpm	60 % = 94 bpm	60 % = 94 bpm	70 % = 110 bpm	____% = ____bpm	60 % = 94 bpm
Body Parts (Listed By Priority)	Body Part Workout 1. ____ × ____ sets 2. ____ × ____ sets 3. ____ × ____ sets 4. ____ × ____ sets 5. ____ × ____ sets	Body Part Workout 1. abdomen × 3 sets 2. waist × 2 sets 3. chest × 1 sets 4. hips × 1 sets 5. shoulders × 0 sets	Body Part Workout 1. abdomen × 1 sets 2. waist × 1 sets 3. chest × 0 sets 4. hips × 0 sets 5. shoulders × 0 sets	Body Part Workout 1. ____ × ____ sets 2. ____ × ____ sets 3. ____ × ____ sets 4. ____ × ____ sets 5. ____ × ____ sets	Body Part Workout 1. abdomen × 2 sets 2. waist × 1 sets 3. chest × 1 sets 4. hips × 1 sets 5. shoulders × 0 sets	Body Part Workout 1. abdomen × 1 sets 2. waist × 2 sets 3. chest × 1 sets 4. hips × 1 sets 5. shoulders × 0 sets	Body Part Workout 1. abdomen × 3 sets 2. waist × 2 sets 3. chest × 1 sets 4. hips × 1 sets 5. shoulders × 0 sets
Cool-Down Exercises	( ) Yes (X) No	(X) Yes ( ) No	(X) Yes ( ) No	(X) Yes ( ) No	(X) Yes ( ) No	(X) Yes ( ) No	(X) Yes ( ) No
Notes/Comments On Today's Workout	Played 18 holes of golf. It went very well. The Warm-Up Exercises may have helped! Walked the entire 18 holes.		For aerobic workout, walked 25 minutes, swam 15 minutes.	Used walking as my aerobic workout.	For aerobic workout, followed Jack's Complete Fat-Burning workout video tape for 20 minutes.		Followed Jack's Low-Impact Aerobics video tape workout, but only did 45 minutes of aerobic workout today. Got behind in my schedule today and never caught up!

My Working Pulse Rate	WEEK 1		
60% = _____bpm **70%** = _____bpm **80%** = _____bpm	**SUNDAY**	**MONDAY**	**TUESDAY**
Resting Pulse Rate	_____ bpm	_____ bpm	_____ bpm
Warm-Up Exercises	( )Yes ( )No	( )Yes ( )No	( )Yes ( )No
Total Scheduled Walking Time (Or Other Aerobic Workout)	Aerobic Workout **REST DAY**	Aerobic Workout	Aerobic Workout **40 min.**
Working Heart Rate	_____% = _____bpm	_____% = _____bpm	60 % = _____bpm
Body Parts (Listed By Priority)	Body Part Workout 1._____ × _____ sets 2._____ × _____ sets 3._____ × _____ sets 4._____ × _____ sets 5._____ × _____ sets	Body Part Workout 1._____ × 3 sets 2._____ × 2 sets 3._____ × 1 sets 4._____ × 1 sets 5._____ × 0 sets	Body Part Workout 1._____ × 1 sets 2._____ × 1 sets 3._____ × 0 sets 4._____ × 0 sets 5._____ × 0 sets
Cool-Down Exercises	( )Yes ( )No	( )Yes ( )No	( )Yes ( )No
Notes/Comments On Today's Workout			

The One-Week Trial Run

WEDNESDAY	THURSDAY	FRIDAY	SATURDAY
_____ bpm	_____ bpm	_____ bpm	_____ bpm
( )Yes ( )No	( )Yes ( )No	( )Yes ( )No	( )Yes ( )No
Aerobic Workout	Aerobic Workout	Aerobic Workout	Aerobic Workout
20 min.	**20 min.**		**60 min.**
_60_ % = _____bpm	_70_ % = _____bpm	____% = _____bpm	_60_ % = _____bpm
Body Part Workout	Body Part Workout	Body Part Workout	Body Part Workout
1._____ × _____ sets 2._____ × _____ sets 3._____ × _____ sets 4._____ × _____ sets 5._____ × _____ sets	1._____ × 2 sets 2._____ × 1 sets 3._____ × 1 sets 4._____ × 1 sets 5._____ × 0 sets	1._____ × 1 sets 2._____ × 2 sets 3._____ × 1 sets 4._____ × 1 sets 5._____ × 0 sets	1._____ × 3 sets 2._____ × 2 sets 3._____ × 1 sets 4._____ × 1 sets 5._____ × 0 sets
( )Yes ( )No	( )Yes ( )No	( )Yes ( )No	( )Yes ( )No

EVALUATING YOUR TEST

At the conclusion of the one-week trial period, with your filled-in program in front of you, review the week as objectively as possible. Ask the following questions:

1. Am I unusually tired after the ambitious Saturday workout?
2. Will taking today as a rest day provide adequate recovery time so that I will be ready to begin another week's worth of exercise?
3. Were there any days in the past week when the scheduled workouts were too much for my current state of fitness?
4. Did I overestimate my readiness to embark on this program?
5. Which days in the week were the most pleasant, the more difficult days or the physically easier days?
6. Did the hard/easy aspect of the week provide me with enough time to recover from the previous day's workout?
7. Would I do better with a program based upon hard/easy/easy?
8. Was I unusually tired when I began the aerobic portion of the workout? Or did the aerobic portion of the workout serve as much to relax and invigorate me as it did to increase my endurance?
9. What single thing about the week's program would I change?

Remember that no exercise program is cast in stone. An exercise program that does not seem to be working for you personally may be falling short for any one of a number of reasons:

1. Perhaps you overestimated your ability to do the workouts called for and you may have come to it inadequately trained. In this case, drop back to your former program and gradually build it to the point where you are strong enough to take on the new program, then re-enter the new program at the beginning.

2. You may be strong in one of the two essential areas (aerobic or body part) and relatively weak in the other. If so, again drop back in your program and gradually build up the area that is weak. When you are satisfied that the area that was wanting is now adequate, embark again on the new program. Remember that this program is based on strength training and a balance of aerobic fitness and body part development.

3. You may be prepared for the new program, but feel that you need two rest days a week. Modify your program to reflect that. But don't make too many modifications or you'll lose the maximum benefit. If you need an extra rest day, take Wednesday off in addition to Sunday. That way you will not give up a day of body parts workouts, and you will not go more than two days without an aerobics workout.

The two most common problems encountered in taking on a new program are these:

1. Basic preparation has been inadequate and the body is not yet ready to embark on the full program because there is a deficiency in either the aerobic or the body parts side of the base program. (This is often due to a person who works out with a friend assuming that both are progressing at the same rate, and when the friend wants to begin a new program, the friend's partner wants to go along with it, even though inadequately prepared.)

2. The exerciser feels the new program is too easy and begins adding some additional workouts. (This can undermine the entire program by causing the exerciser to go into a difficult workout session while still recovering from the last tough workout.)

The exerciser *must* learn to read his or her body properly. If you are tired the day after a particularly difficult workout day, admit it to yourself. Remember, you're not invincible. Maybe you didn't get adequate sleep the night before. If you find this happening, drop back to your regular exercising and reschedule the week's program for sometime next month. This exercise program isn't designed to put a great deal of pressure on you so that it causes you to lose sleep. An exercise program should be a way of relaxing and enjoying the process of becoming and staying fit. It should be a source of stress-release, not a source of stress.

Now that you've evaluated your body's (and your mind's) reaction to the week's program, take a moment to plot your Resting Pulse Rate for the week. Simply take a piece of paper and copy down the Resting Pulse Rates from Sunday to Saturday from the week past. Now, add Sunday of this week.

If everything went as planned, you should find that the lowest pulse rate for the week was Monday morning, and the highest was either Friday or Sunday of this week. The higher Resting Pulse Rate is an indication that your body is working hard to recover from a hard workout on the previous day.

If the highest Resting Pulse Rate comes on a day other than Friday or Sunday, backtrack in your mind to check if you did any additional work on the day before the high Resting Pulse Rate reading, such as garden work, shopping all day, vacuuming, extra housework, etc. An elevated Resting Pulse Rate (and by elevated, we mean 4-10 beats above your current normal) can also be a reaction to stress. Did you have a particularly stressful day the day before the elevated reading? Did you receive some bad news that caused you to have a sleepless night? These are all factors that can cause the Resting Pulse Rate to become elevated.

If your week was a relatively normal week, however, your Resting Pulse Rate will typically rise in the wake of the more ambitious workouts, and then will decline after the body has repaired itself.

There are some cautions that you should keep in mind.

If you have completed the week of exercising and you find that your Resting Pulse Rate is erratic for the week, that it has gone up and stayed up, you may not be ready for this ambitious a program. If this is the case, drop back and work gradually on your individual aerobic program and your individual body parts programs, increasing their intensity very, very gradually until you are at a strong base level.

If you are experiencing unusual soreness or stiffness, you may not be ready. Cut your body parts exercises in half for the next week, and take your time in doing your exercises. Also, remember that it is very important to faithfully do your Warm-Up and Cool-Down exercises. That is why there is a box on each day's program so you can mark whether or not you did the Warm-up and Cool-Down exercises. If you go headlong into an exercise program without adequate Warm-Up, you can easily become stiff and sore. Do those Warm-Up exercises faithfully. And the same goes for the Cool-Down exercises. They are very important for cooling down your muscles, and also for gradually cooling down your heart.

A word of caution here. Make haste slowly. It has also been my experience that some people who get into exercise get so enthusiastic about the wonderful changes in their bodies (and in their minds) that they tend to feel they are capable of things their bodies are not really capable of yet. If you try to objectively evaluate yourself, and there is any question in your mind concerning your abilities, do half of what you think you can do. Better you should be behind your best friend on the programs in this book than to be stiff and sore.

If you feel you have seen improvement in yourself this week, move on to Chapter 7. If not, repeat this week.

The One-Month Preview Program

With a week's workout comfortably behind you, it is time to move to the one-month program.

The reason we don't use the one-week trial run as a springboard to a six-month program is that it is too huge a leap and can be intimidating to most people. You wouldn't step from the bottom rung of a ladder to the top without taking each rung one at a time. By practicing on a month's program, you can evaluate your readiness to make a further commitment.

You will begin to appreciate the hard/easy aspect and the variety in such a program.

When I begin discussing this step of the program with ambitious exercisers, the first question I usually get is this: "Which month is the best month to use as my preview month?"

My typical response is this: "Don't wait for too long following your *successful* week-long trial run."

The reason I feel that you should not wait too long is that to wait too long is to have the good effects and the positive memories of the one-week program wear off. You've now seen the good results of such a program. Keep your momentum going.

As you saw with the one-week program, I always like to set up the weeks in the traditional way, with Sunday as the first day. I also like to leave Sunday as a Rest Day because people generally have so many things of a non-exercise nature to do on that day. However, it really depends upon your schedule and what works best for you. You might want to do at least your Warm-Up exercises on Sunday just to stay limber.

You need not schedule this month's exercises precisely covering a month on a calendar page. If you feel like beginning on the third week of one month, then continue into the next month.

Let's once again review the important elements: hard/easy, variety, and rest.

Hard/easy: If you were to study the one-month program that follows, you would quickly see that just as the individual days are set up as hard or easy days, so are the weeks in this month. The first week is relatively easy. Then the second week becomes more difficult. The third week is still more difficult. But then the fourth week drops back and is as easy as the first week. This method takes the hard/easy theory and applies it to an entire month. There is a build-up in exertion, and then a drop-off to provide a rest period before the next build-up. (When we get to the six-month program, you will be able to see how this pattern works on an extended basis as well as on a monthly and even daily basis.)

Unlike the week-long program, you will also notice that in the month-long schedule, a fifth line has been added to the box that lists your body part priorities. This line is for you to work in a fifth problem zone, if needed. Start this fifth body part on the 1st Level, gradually increasing to the 2nd Level as it feels comfortable.

Variety: The addition of the fifth body part will add a bit of variety to your body part workout. But don't be afraid to add variety to your aerobic side, too. If you have been using Dynastriding as your aerobic exercise, perhaps you'll want to work aerobicly on a stationary bicycle, or perhaps you'll want to attempt jogging instead of Dynastriding. Be creative, both to keep yourself interested in the workouts by providing variety, and to use various muscle groups. Remember to follow the guidelines for the time and the effort (see Working Heart Rate, page 89).

Rest: Rest is an essential ingredient in any exercise program. If you are feeling a bit tired from the workouts, don't be afraid to take Wednesday as an additional Rest Day.

SOME CAUTIONS WHILE ENGAGING IN THIS PROGRAM

The more you exercise, the more you should be capable of monitoring your body's reaction to the exercise. Are you unusually tired after a hard day's workout? Is it taking you longer than usual to recover? Is your Resting Pulse Rate in the morning unusually high? If you feel you are overdoing it, back off immediately.

Either drop back to the workouts in the previous week until you are comfortable doing them, or if it is just too much, drop back to your regular workouts and put the one-month preview program off until you feel you are ready to do it comfortably. Remember: Exercising should revive you, not leave you panting and exhausted. If you are exhausted, you're doing too much too soon. If you don't back off, you'll either end up hating your exercising or you'll end up injuring or exhausting yourself, *and then* you'll hate exercising.

A fitness program is designed to help you, not to hurt you. Keep that in mind.

If you feel you're ready for The One-Month Preview Program, go to it!

WEEK 1

My Working Pulse Rate	SUNDAY	MONDAY	TUESDAY
60% = _____ bpm 70% = _____ bpm 80% = _____ bpm			
Resting Pulse Rate	_____ bpm	_____ bpm	_____ bpm
Warm-Up Exercises	( )Yes ( )No	( )Yes ( )No	( )Yes ( )No
Total Scheduled Walking Time (Or Other Aerobic Workout)	Aerobic Workout REST DAY	Aerobic Workout 	Aerobic Workout 40 min.
Working Heart Rate	_____ % = _____ bpm	_____ % = _____ bpm	60 % = _____ bpm
Body Parts (Listed By Priority)	Body Part Workout 1.____ × ____ sets 2.____ × ____ sets 3.____ × ____ sets 4.____ × ____ sets 5.____ × ____ sets	Body Part Workout 1.____ × 2 sets 2.____ × 2 sets 3.____ × 2 sets 4.____ × 1 sets 5.____ × 1 sets	Body Part Workout 1.____ × 1 sets 2.____ × 1 sets 3.____ × 1 sets 4.____ × 0 sets 5.____ × 0 sets
Cool-Down Exercises	( )Yes ( )No	( )Yes ( )No	( )Yes ( )No
Notes/Comments On Today's Workout			

The One-Month Preview Program

WEDNESDAY	THURSDAY	FRIDAY	SATURDAY
_____ bpm	_____ bpm	_____ bpm	_____ bpm
( )Yes ( )No	( )Yes ( )No	( )Yes ( )No	( )Yes ( )No
Aerobic Workout	Aerobic Workout	Aerobic Workout	Aerobic Workout
20 min.	**25 min.**		**60 min.**
_60_ % = _____bpm	_70_ % = _____bpm	____ % = _____bpm	_60_ % = _____bpm
Body Part Workout	Body Part Workout	Body Part Workout	Body Part Workout
1._____ × _____ sets 2._____ × _____ sets 3._____ × _____ sets 4._____ × _____ sets 5._____ × _____ sets	1._____ × 2 sets 2._____ × 2 sets 3._____ × 1 sets 4._____ × 1 sets 5._____ × 1 sets	1._____ × 1 sets 2._____ × 2 sets 3._____ × 2 sets 4._____ × 2 sets 5._____ × 1 sets	1._____ × 3 sets 2._____ × 2 sets 3._____ × 2 sets 4._____ × 1 sets 5._____ × 1 sets
( )Yes ( )No	( )Yes ( )No	( )Yes ( )No	( )Yes ( )No

The One-Month Preview Program

My Working Pulse Rate	**WEEK 2**		
60% = _____ bpm 70% = _____ bpm 80% = _____ bpm	**SUNDAY**	**MONDAY**	**TUESDAY**
Resting Pulse Rate	_____ bpm	_____ bpm	_____ bpm
Warm-Up Exercises	( )Yes ( )No	( )Yes ( )No	( )Yes ( )No
Total Scheduled Walking Time (Or Other Aerobic Workout)	Aerobic Workout **REST DAY**	Aerobic Workout	Aerobic Workout **45 min.**
Working Heart Rate	_____ % = _____ bpm	_____ % = _____ bpm	70 % = _____ bpm
Body Parts (Listed By Priority)	Body Part Workout 1.____ × ____ sets 2.____ × ____ sets 3.____ × ____ sets 4.____ × ____ sets 5.____ × ____ sets	Body Part Workout 1.____ × 3 sets 2.____ × 2 sets 3.____ × 2 sets 4.____ × 1 sets 5.____ × 1 sets	Body Part Workout 1.____ × 2 sets 2.____ × 1 sets 3.____ × 1 sets 4.____ × 1 sets 5.____ × 0 sets
Cool-Down Exercises	( )Yes ( )No	( )Yes ( )No	( )Yes ( )No
Notes/Comments On Today's Workout			

WEDNESDAY	THURSDAY	FRIDAY	SATURDAY
_____ bpm	_____ bpm	_____ bpm	_____ bpm
( )Yes ( )No	( )Yes ( )No	( )Yes ( )No	( )Yes ( )No
Aerobic Workout	Aerobic Workout	Aerobic Workout	Aerobic Workout
25 min.	30 min.		60 min.
_60_ % = _____ bpm	_70_ % = _____ bpm	_____ % = _____ bpm	_70_ % = _____ bpm
Body Part Workout	Body Part Workout	Body Part Workout	Body Part Workout
1._____ × _____ sets 2._____ × _____ sets 3._____ × _____ sets 4._____ × _____ sets 5._____ × _____ sets	1._____ × 2 sets 2._____ × 2 sets 3._____ × 1 sets 4._____ × 1 sets 5._____ × 1 sets	1._____ × 1 sets 2._____ × 2 sets 3._____ × 3 sets 4._____ × 2 sets 5._____ × 1 sets	1._____ × 2 sets 2._____ × 2 sets 3._____ × 2 sets 4._____ × 1 sets 5._____ × 1 sets
( )Yes ( )No	( )Yes ( )No	( )Yes ( )No	( )Yes ( )No

My Working Pulse Rate	WEEK 3		
60% = _____ bpm **70%** = _____ bpm **80%** = _____ bpm	**SUNDAY**	**MONDAY**	**TUESDAY**
Resting Pulse Rate	_____ bpm	_____ bpm	_____ bpm
Warm-Up Exercises	( )Yes ( )No	( )Yes ( )No	( )Yes ( )No
Total Scheduled Walking Time (Or Other Aerobic Workout)	Aerobic Workout **REST DAY**	Aerobic Workout	Aerobic Workout **45 min.**
Working Heart Rate	_____ % = _____ bpm	_____ % = _____ bpm	_70_ % = _____ bpm
Body Parts (Listed By Priority)	Body Part Workout 1. ____ × ____ sets 2. ____ × ____ sets 3. ____ × ____ sets 4. ____ × ____ sets 5. ____ × ____ sets	Body Part Workout 1. ____ × 3 sets 2. ____ × 3 sets 3. ____ × 2 sets 4. ____ × 2 sets 5. ____ × 1 sets	Body Part Workout 1. ____ × 2 sets 2. ____ × 2 sets 3. ____ × 1 sets 4. ____ × 1 sets 5. ____ × 1 sets
Cool-Down Exercises	( )Yes ( )No	( )Yes ( )No	( )Yes ( )No
Notes/Comments On Today's Workout			

The One-Month Preview Program

WEDNESDAY	THURSDAY	FRIDAY	SATURDAY
_____ bpm	_____ bpm	_____ bpm	_____ bpm
( )Yes ( )No	( )Yes ( )No	( )Yes ( )No	( )Yes ( )No
Aerobic Workout	Aerobic Workout	Aerobic Workout	Aerobic Workout
30 min.	30 min.		60 min.
60 % = _____ bpm	70 % = _____ bpm	____ % = _____ bpm	70 % = _____ bpm
Body Part Workout	Body Part Workout	Body Part Workout	Body Part Workout
1.____ × ____ sets 2.____ × ____ sets 3.____ × ____ sets 4.____ × ____ sets 5.____ × ____ sets	1.____ × 2 sets 2.____ × 2 sets 3.____ × 2 sets 4.____ × 1 sets 5.____ × 1 sets	1.____ × 1 sets 2.____ × 2 sets 3.____ × 3 sets 4.____ × 2 sets 5.____ × 1 sets	1.____ × 3 sets 2.____ × 3 sets 3.____ × 2 sets 4.____ × 2 sets 5.____ × 1 sets
( )Yes ( )No	( )Yes ( )No	( )Yes ( )No	( )Yes ( )No

My Working Pulse Rate	SUNDAY ·	MONDAY	TUESDAY
60% = _____ bpm **70%** = _____ bpm **80%** = _____ bpm			
Resting Pulse Rate	_____ bpm	_____ bpm	_____ bpm
Warm-Up Exercises	( )Yes ( )No	( )Yes ( )No	( )Yes ( )No
Total Scheduled Walking Time (Or Other Aerobic Workout)	Aerobic Workout **REST DAY**	Aerobic Workout 	Aerobic Workout **30 min.**
Working Heart Rate	____% = _____ bpm	____% = _____ bpm	60 % = _____ bpm
Body Parts (Listed By Priority)	Body Part Workout 1.____×____ sets 2.____×____ sets 3.____×____ sets 4.____×____ sets 5.____×____ sets	Body Part Workout 1.____× 2 sets 2.____× 2 sets 3.____× 2 sets 4.____× 2 sets 5.____× 1 sets	Body Part Workout 1.____× 1 sets 2.____× 1 sets 3.____× 1 sets 4.____× 1 sets 5.____× 0 sets
Cool-Down Exercises	( )Yes ( )No	( )Yes ( )No	( )Yes ( )No
Notes/Comments On Today's Workout			

The One-Month Preview Program

WEDNESDAY	THURSDAY	FRIDAY	SATURDAY
_____ bpm	_____ bpm	_____ bpm	_____ bpm
( )Yes ( )No	( )Yes ( )No	( )Yes ( )No	( )Yes ( )No
Aerobic Workout	Aerobic Workout	Aerobic Workout	Aerobic Workout
20 min.	**30 min.**		**60 min.**
60 % = _____ bpm	70 % = _____ bpm	___ % = _____ bpm	60 % = _____ bpm
Body Part Workout	Body Part Workout	Body Part Workout	Body Part Workout
1._____ × _____ sets 2._____ × _____ sets 3._____ × _____ sets 4._____ × _____ sets 5._____ × _____ sets	1._____ × 2 sets 2._____ × 2 sets 3._____ × 1 sets 4._____ × 1 sets 5._____ × 1 sets	1._____ × 2 sets 2._____ × 2 sets 3._____ × 2 sets 4._____ × 1 sets 5._____ × 1 sets	1._____ × 2 sets 2._____ × 2 sets 3._____ × 2 sets 4._____ × 1 sets 5._____ × 1 sets
( )Yes ( )No	( )Yes ( )No	( )Yes ( )No	( )Yes ( )No

AT THE CONCLUSION OF THE MONTH

Just as you did for the the One-Week Trial Run, let's take some time to evaluate your month-long exercise program.

1. Resting Pulse Rate. The longer the exercise program, the more accurate a guideline the Resting Pulse Rate becomes. I usually like to make a little graph and then plot my RPR (Resting Pulse Rate) for the month. That quickly points out any peaks, which are of much more concern than valleys. (If you have been exercising aerobically for some time, your pulse rate should have fallen somewhat and then leveled off. Over the years, your RPR may continue to fall, but at a much slower rate than it did within the first six months of your aerobic fitness.)

Peaks in the RPR indicate that, for some reason, the body is working hard to maintain or repair itself. A 5-10 point increase in the RPR can be due to unusual stress or tension in your life or it can be due to an illness (especially something like a bout with the flu). It can also be a reaction to a particularly difficult workout the day before.

Go back over your month's workouts and see if the peaks in your RPR chart correspond with hard workouts the day before, or if they correspond with particularly trying times in your month, or with periods where you were ill. (This is where the bottom box on a day's workout—that reserved for Notes/Comments—comes into play. For instance, if you jotted down in the Notes/Comments box for Wednesday of the third week that you had a touch of the flu, and your RPR for Wednesday and Thursday is elevated, the mystery is solved.)

If your RPR is high several days in a row and there is no logical explanation for it, you may be overtraining. In other words, you may have begun the month-long program without really being ready for it.

You may want to back off a bit and take on the month-long challenge once you are in better shape.

2. Objectively evaluate any aches and pains. It is perfectly understandable, for instance, to experience some fairly noticeable aches in the wake of the first, second, and even third sessions when you begin working on body parts you have not worked on before. Also, it is normal to experience sore muscles if you neglected your workouts for one reason or another. Workouts should not be chronically painful, and the aches should eventually go away on their own as your body becomes increasingly acquainted with the workouts expected of it. Pay special attention to any sharp pains or persistent pains. Aches are usually normal: they indicate that your muscles are doing work to which they are unaccustomed. Acute pains are not normal, so check with your doctor if they persist.

Some people who have been physically inactive most of their lives are unaccustomed to any kind of physical aches, and become alarmed, especially at first. However, you'll eventually develop a certain insight into your own body, and you can tell pretty well whether you are experiencing a typical exercising ache or a pain that indicates you've overdone it.

If it's a legitimate pain, back down from your exercising.

After you've evaluated your month-long program and feel you're ready for a way of life program, move on to Chapter 8.

A Year In Your Life: Six Months At A Time

You eat every day, sleep every day, brush your teeth every day, your body was made to move every day! So, let's move into a way of life today, and move into the six-month program of reshaping your body through the hard/easy philosophy.

This allows the exerciser to constantly go through periods of building and recuperation, building and recuperation, on a weekly, monthly, six-month, and ultimately yearly basis.

He who hesitates is lost. I find that if I don't get into something when I'm thinking of it, pretty soon I'm no longer thinking of it and I forget to get myself excited about it again unless someone reminds me.

ANOTHER LOOK AT THE THREE MOST IMPORTANT FACTORS

As we've done with the week- and month-long programs, let's consider the three prime factors:

Hard/easy: We've already discussed how the days of the week are set up in a hard/easy format to provide for work and then for recuperation. We saw in the last chapter how this theory is applied to the month-long workout. In the six-month program, there are five months of gradual build-up (with hard/easy in every week and month), and then there is a recuperative drop

back to nearly your starting level. From there, you could repeat the six-month program and begin to once again build.

The muscles must work and then they must recuperate, work and then recuperate.

As you've probably observed by watching nature, the yearly cycle works much like that: in spring plants bloom, in summer they grow, in autumn they begin to back off, and in winter they rest. Then the cycle begins again.

Variety: Suggestions for a varied workout:

1. Occasionally substitute in another aerobic activity for your prime aerobic activity. For instance, if you are Dynastriding as your primary aerobic activity, why not occasionally substitute bicycle riding, aerobic dance, or swimming? Or, in the winter, why not substitute cross-country skiing?

2. If the weather outside is pleasant, take your Body Part Specific workouts as well as your Warm-Up and Cool-Down exercises outside. Spread a little exercise mat or a blanket on the balcony or the grass in the backyard and do your exercising outdoors.

3. Don't overlook your exercise program if you travel. When we travel—and we travel quite a bit each year—Jack rearranges the hotel room so that he can do his circuit-training workout each morning. Be creative. Continuing your exercise pro-

gram on a trip or at a relative's house adds to the variety factor. Go with it, enjoy it.

4. Use the buddy system. Invite a friend to take part in your fitness program. If you are scheduled for a 30-minute walk on Monday and a friend is fit enough to keep up with you, why not invite that friend along?

Rest: The need for rest is important, both in your daily life and in the pursuit of fitness. Get good, solid sleep. When you engage in a regular exercise program, you'll likely feel more energized all day long, but you may also experience sleeping patterns that you haven't enjoyed in many years. When you become sleepy, go to bed. As you get more and more into your program, you may find yourself going to bed at an earlier hour and getting better quality sleep, and perhaps waking up later. Just go with what your body seems to want. It knows best what kind of rest it needs. A good night's sleep is frequently a byproduct of a regular exercise program.

CAUTIONS

1. If you begin to feel as though the program is too much for you, don't be afraid to retreat. By dropping back, you may be able to recover enough so that you can continue.

2. If your program is interrupted by illness, drop back in your program and restart. This will make provisions for your body to recuperate properly.

3. If your program is interrupted by travel or by visitors, make provisions to exercise while traveling or while entertaining company. While traveling, it can be a refreshing change to work your program into your new environment. And if you have company at the house, they will certainly understand your absence for an hour or two while you exercise to improve yourself and they may even join you in your workout.

A NOTE FOR THOSE INTERESTED ONLY IN BODY PART WORKOUTS

Although this program was designed to improve the shape, tone, and muscle endurance of various body parts in conjunction with an ongoing aerobic-based fitness program, the program *can* be used without the aerobics portion.

For the record, I do not advise doing merely the body part exercises, because, as I stated previ-

ously, the heart is the body's most important muscle, and it should be strengthened first, foremost, and continuously.

For an exerciser who wishes to take advantage of only the body part exercises, the program will work if you drop all of the aerobics portions from each day's schedule. It is doubly important for those using only the body part workouts to use an ambitious set of Warm-Up and Cool-Down exercises before and after your exercise session! In fact, if you want to use only the body part exercises, I would advise that instead of using only five Warm-Up and five Cool-Down exercises, as outlined in Part II, do a dozen Warm-Up and Cool-Down exercises.

This will impart a better general muscle fitness, and will more thoroughly avoid muscle, joint, tendon, and ligament soreness, all of which will be more prone to the body that is not engaged in a general aerobic fitness program.

If you want to begin taking up an aerobic fitness program, I believe that walking is the best and easiest. You might want to consult my previous book, *DYNASTRIDE!*, for a complete program.

BODY PART CONSIDERATIONS

You are completely in charge of the Body Parts Specific portion of this program.

You will find that there is always space listed for five body parts. It becomes too complicated and too exhausting if you attempt to take on more than that. However, you are entirely in charge of which body parts you are working on at any time in your program. My suggestion is that every two months you take an objective look at the progress or lack of progress on your list of body part priorities. If number 1 has shown great improvement but number 3 has shown little improvement, merely move them around on your list, making number 3 into number 1, and perhaps moving what had been number 1 down to number 4.

You are in charge of moving body parts around in your priority list and you are in charge of taking body parts off and putting new ones on. I would bear in mind, however, that although the Warm-Up and Cool-Down exercises work a great number of the body parts, they do not generally provide enough specific workout to any one part to maintain it if it has been a problem body part. Therefore, I would always keep my original number 1 priority body part on the exercise list of five body parts, but as it improves, I would gradually move it down the list until it reaches a spot where it is being maintained adequately.

You'll probably be making adjustments up and down the priority list; that's the beauty of this program. Besides providing basic fitness and adequate aerobic fitness, it also lends itself to being customized to provide first-class fitness for whatever body parts you feel need work.

PREVIEW OF THINGS TO COME

At the beginning of this section, we spoke about a way of life.

I think you can see that we're getting very close to it. The week and the month trial programs were previews. The six-month program is the basic structure. In the next chapter, we'll explore the ways you can continually customize the program you are about to experience to meet your individual needs for the rest of your life.

Now, on to a lifetime worth of fun and fitness—and a new body for you. You've earned it!

My Working Pulse Rate	WEEK 1		
60% = _____ bpm **70%** = _____ bpm **80%** = _____ bpm			
	SUNDAY	**MONDAY**	**TUESDAY**
Resting Pulse Rate	_____ bpm	_____ bpm	_____ bpm
Warm-Up Exercises	( )Yes ( )No	( )Yes ( )No	( )Yes ( )No
Total Scheduled Walking Time (Or Other Aerobic Workout)	Aerobic Workout **REST DAY**	Aerobic Workout	Aerobic Workout **45 min.**
Working Heart Rate	_____ % = _____ bpm	_____ % = _____ bpm	70 % = _____ bpm
Body Parts (Listed By Priority)	Body Part Workout 1._____ × _____ sets 2._____ × _____ sets 3._____ × _____ sets 4._____ × _____ sets 5._____ × _____ sets	Body Part Workout 1._____ × 3 sets 2._____ × 2 sets 3._____ × 2 sets 4._____ × 1 sets 5._____ × 1 sets	Body Part Workout 1._____ × 2 sets 2._____ × 1 sets 3._____ × 1 sets 4._____ × 1 sets 5._____ × 0 sets
Cool-Down Exercises	( )Yes ( )No	( )Yes ( )No	( )Yes ( )No
Notes/Comments On Today's Workout			

A Half Year In Your Life . . .

WEDNESDAY	THURSDAY	FRIDAY	SATURDAY
_____ bpm	_____ bpm	_____ bpm	_____ bpm
( )Yes ( )No	( )Yes ( )No	( )Yes ( )No	( )Yes ( )No
Aerobic Workout	Aerobic Workout	Aerobic Workout	Aerobic Workout
25 min.	30 min.		60 min.
_60_ % = _____bpm	_70_ % = _____bpm	____ % = _____bpm	_70_ % = _____bpm
Body Part Workout	Body Part Workout	Body Part Workout	Body Part Workout
1.____ × ____ sets 2.____ × ____ sets 3.____ × ____ sets 4.____ × ____ sets 5.____ × ____ sets	1.____ × 2 sets 2.____ × 2 sets 3.____ × 1 sets 4.____ × 1 sets 5.____ × 1 sets	1.____ × 1 sets 2.____ × 2 sets 3.____ × 3 sets 4.____ × 2 sets 5.____ × 1 sets	1.____ × 2 sets 2.____ × 2 sets 3.____ × 2 sets 4.____ × 1 sets 5.____ × 1 sets
( )Yes ( )No	( )Yes ( )No	( )Yes ( )No	( )Yes ( )No

My Working Pulse Rate	WEEK 2		
60% = _____ bpm **70%** = _____ bpm **80%** = _____ bpm			
	SUNDAY	**MONDAY**	**TUESDAY**
Resting Pulse Rate	_____ bpm	_____ bpm	_____ bpm
Warm-Up Exercises	( )Yes ( )No	( )Yes ( )No	( )Yes ( )No
Total Scheduled Walking Time (Or Other Aerobic Workout)	Aerobic Workout **REST DAY**	Aerobic Workout	Aerobic Workout **45 min.**
Working Heart Rate	____ % = ____ bpm	____ % = ____ bpm	_70_ % = ____ bpm
Body Parts (Listed By Priority)	Body Part Workout 1. ____ × ____ sets 2. ____ × ____ sets 3. ____ × ____ sets 4. ____ × ____ sets 5. ____ × ____ sets	Body Part Workout 1. ____ × 3 sets 2. ____ × 3 sets 3. ____ × 2 sets 4. ____ × 2 sets 5. ____ × 1 sets	Body Part Workout 1. ____ × 2 sets 2. ____ × 2 sets 3. ____ × 1 sets 4. ____ × 1 sets 5. ____ × 1 sets
Cool-Down Exercises	( )Yes ( )No	( )Yes ( )No	( )Yes ( )No
Notes/Comments On Today's Workout			

A Half Year In Your Life . . .

114

WEDNESDAY	THURSDAY	FRIDAY	SATURDAY
_____ bpm	_____ bpm	_____ bpm	_____ bpm
( )Yes ( )No	( )Yes ( )No	( )Yes ( )No	( )Yes ( )No
Aerobic Workout	Aerobic Workout	Aerobic Workout	Aerobic Workout
30 min.	30 min.		60 min.
__60__ % = _____ bpm	__70__ % = _____ bpm	_____ % = _____ bpm	__70__ % = _____ bpm
Body Part Workout	Body Part Workout	Body Part Workout	Body Part Workout
1.____ × ____ sets 2.____ × ____ sets 3.____ × ____ sets 4.____ × ____ sets 5.____ × ____ sets	1.____ × 2 sets 2.____ × 2 sets 3.____ × 2 sets 4.____ × 1 sets 5.____ × 1 sets	1.____ × 1 sets 2.____ × 2 sets 3.____ × 3 sets 4.____ × 2 sets 5.____ × 1 sets	1.____ × 3 sets 2.____ × 3 sets 3.____ × 2 sets 4.____ × 2 sets 5.____ × 1 sets
( )Yes ( )No	( )Yes ( )No	( )Yes ( )No	( )Yes ( )No

My Working Pulse Rate	SUNDAY	MONDAY	TUESDAY
60% = _____ bpm 70% = _____ bpm 80% = _____ bpm			
Resting Pulse Rate	_____ bpm	_____ bpm	_____ bpm
Warm-Up Exercises	( )Yes ( )No	( )Yes ( )No	( )Yes ( )No
Total Scheduled Walking Time (Or Other Aerobic Workout)	Aerobic Workout **REST DAY**	Aerobic Workout	Aerobic Workout **45 min.**
Working Heart Rate	_____% = _____ bpm	_____% = _____ bpm	70 % = _____ bpm
Body Parts (Listed By Priority)	Body Part Workout 1.____ × ____ sets 2.____ × ____ sets 3.____ × ____ sets 4.____ × ____ sets 5.____ × ____ sets	Body Part Workout 1.____ × 4 sets 2.____ × 3 sets 3.____ × 2 sets 4.____ × 2 sets 5.____ × 1 sets	Body Part Workout 1.____ × 3 sets 2.____ × 2 sets 3.____ × 1 sets 4.____ × 1 sets 5.____ × 0 sets
Cool-Down Exercises	( )Yes ( )No	( )Yes ( )No	( )Yes ( )No
Notes/Comments On Today's Workout			

A Half Year In Your Life . . .

WEDNESDAY	THURSDAY	FRIDAY	SATURDAY
_____ bpm	_____ bpm	_____ bpm	_____ bpm
( )Yes ( )No	( )Yes ( )No	( )Yes ( )No	( )Yes ( )No
Aerobic Workout	Aerobic Workout	Aerobic Workout	Aerobic Workout
30 min.	40 min.		70 min.
_60_ % = _____bpm	_70_ % = _____bpm	_____ % = _____bpm	_60_ % = _____bpm
Body Part Workout	Body Part Workout	Body Part Workout	Body Part Workout
1.____ × ____ sets 2.____ × ____ sets 3.____ × ____ sets 4.____ × ____ sets 5.____ × ____ sets	1.____ × 3 sets 2.____ × 2 sets 3.____ × 2 sets 4.____ × 1 sets 5.____ × 1 sets	1.____ × 1 sets 2.____ × 2 sets 3.____ × 3 sets 4.____ × 2 sets 5.____ × 1 sets	1.____ × 3 sets 2.____ × 3 sets 3.____ × 2 sets 4.____ × 2 sets 5.____ × 1 sets
( )Yes ( )No	( )Yes ( )No	( )Yes ( )No	( )Yes ( )No

My Working Pulse Rate	WEEK 4		
60% = _____ bpm **70%** = _____ bpm **80%** = _____ bpm	**SUNDAY**	**MONDAY**	**TUESDAY**
Resting Pulse Rate	_____ bpm	_____ bpm	_____ bpm
Warm-Up Exercises	( )Yes ( )No	( )Yes ( )No	( )Yes ( )No
Total Scheduled Walking Time (Or Other Aerobic Workout)	Aerobic Workout **REST DAY**	Aerobic Workout	Aerobic Workout **45 min.**
Working Heart Rate	_____% = _____ bpm	_____% = _____ bpm	_____% = _____ bpm
Body Parts (Listed By Priority)	Body Part Workout 1._____ × _____ sets 2._____ × _____ sets 3._____ × _____ sets 4._____ × _____ sets 5._____ × _____ sets	Body Part Workout 1._____ × 3 sets 2._____ × 2 sets 3._____ × 2 sets 4._____ × 1 sets 5._____ × 1 sets	Body Part Workout 1._____ × 2 sets 2._____ × 1 sets 3._____ × 1 sets 4._____ × 1 sets 5._____ × 0 sets
Cool-Down Exercises	( )Yes ( )No	( )Yes ( )No	( )Yes ( )No
Notes/Comments On Today's Workout			

A Half Year In Your Life . . . .

WEDNESDAY	THURSDAY	FRIDAY	SATURDAY
_____ bpm	_____ bpm	_____ bpm	_____ bpm
( )Yes ( )No	( )Yes ( )No	( )Yes ( )No	( )Yes ( )No
Aerobic Workout	Aerobic Workout	Aerobic Workout	Aerobic Workout
25 min.	**30 min.**		**60 min.**
60 % = _____ bpm	70 % = _____ bpm	___ % = _____ bpm	70 % = _____ bpm
Body Part Workout	Body Part Workout	Body Part Workout	Body Part Workout
1._____ × _____ sets 2._____ × _____ sets 3._____ × _____ sets 4._____ × _____ sets 5._____ × _____ sets	1._____ × 2 sets 2._____ × 2 sets 3._____ × 1 sets 4._____ × 1 sets 5._____ × 1 sets	1._____ × 1 sets 2._____ × 2 sets 3._____ × 3 sets 4._____ × 2 sets 5._____ × 1 sets	1._____ × 2 sets 2._____ × 2 sets 3._____ × 2 sets 4._____ × 1 sets 5._____ × 1 sets
( )Yes ( )No	( )Yes ( )No	( )Yes ( )No	( )Yes ( )No

My Working Pulse Rate			
60% = _____ bpm
70% = _____ bpm
80% = _____ bpm			

WEEK 5

	SUNDAY	MONDAY	TUESDAY
Resting Pulse Rate	_____ bpm	_____ bpm	_____ bpm
Warm-Up Exercises	( )Yes
( )No	( )Yes
( )No	( )Yes
( )No
Total Scheduled Walking Time (Or Other Aerobic Workout)	Aerobic Workout

REST DAY | Aerobic Workout | Aerobic Workout

45 min. |
| Working Heart Rate | _____ % = _____ bpm | _____ % = _____ bpm | 70 % = _____ bpm |
| Body Parts (Listed By Priority) | Body Part Workout

1._____ × _____ sets
2._____ × _____ sets
3._____ × _____ sets
4._____ × _____ sets
5._____ × _____ sets | Body Part Workout

1._____ × 3 sets
2._____ × 3 sets
3._____ × 2 sets
4._____ × 2 sets
5._____ × 1 sets | Body Part Workout

1._____ × 3 sets
2._____ × 2 sets
3._____ × 1 sets
4._____ × 1 sets
5._____ × 1 sets |
| Cool-Down Exercises | ( )Yes
( )No | ( )Yes
( )No | ( )Yes
( )No |
| Notes/Comments On Today's Workout | | | |

A Half Year In Your Life . . .

WEDNESDAY	THURSDAY	FRIDAY	SATURDAY
_____ bpm	_____ bpm	_____ bpm	_____ bpm
( )Yes ( )No	( )Yes ( )No	( )Yes ( )No	( )Yes ( )No
Aerobic Workout	Aerobic Workout	Aerobic Workout	Aerobic Workout
30 min.	**30 min.**		**60 min.**
60 % = _____ bpm	70 % = _____ bpm	_____ % = _____ bpm	70 % = _____ bpm
Body Part Workout	Body Part Workout	Body Part Workout	Body Part Workout
1._____ × _____ sets 2._____ × _____ sets 3._____ × _____ sets 4._____ × _____ sets 5._____ × _____ sets	1._____ × 2 sets 2._____ × 2 sets 3._____ × 2 sets 4._____ × 1 sets 5._____ × 1 sets	1._____ × 1 sets 2._____ × 2 sets 3._____ × 3 sets 4._____ × 2 sets 5._____ × 1 sets	1._____ × 3 sets 2._____ × 3 sets 3._____ × 2 sets 4._____ × 2 sets 5._____ × 1 sets
( )Yes ( )No	( )Yes ( )No	( )Yes ( )No	( )Yes ( )No

My Working Pulse Rate			
60% = _____ bpm			
70% = _____ bpm	# WEEK 6		
80% = _____ bpm	**SUNDAY**	**MONDAY**	**TUESDAY**
Resting Pulse Rate	_____ bpm	_____ bpm	_____ bpm
Warm-Up Exercises	( )Yes ( )No	( )Yes ( )No	( )Yes ( )No
Total Scheduled Walking Time (Or Other Aerobic Workout)	Aerobic Workout **REST DAY**	Aerobic Workout 	Aerobic Workout **45 min.**
Working Heart Rate	_____% = _____ bpm	_____% = _____ bpm	_70_ % = _____ bpm
Body Parts (Listed By Priority)	Body Part Workout 1.____ × ____ sets 2.____ × ____ sets 3.____ × ____ sets 4.____ × ____ sets 5.____ × ____ sets	Body Part Workout 1.____ × 4 sets 2.____ × 3 sets 3.____ × 2 sets 4.____ × 2 sets 5.____ × 1 sets	Body Part Workout 1.____ × 3 sets 2.____ × 2 sets 3.____ × 1 sets 4.____ × 1 sets 5.____ × 0 sets
Cool-Down Exercises	( )Yes ( )No	( )Yes ( )No	( )Yes ( )No
Notes/Comments On Today's Workout			

A Half Year In Your Life . . .

WEDNESDAY	THURSDAY	FRIDAY	SATURDAY
_____ bpm	_____ bpm	_____ bpm	_____ bpm
( )Yes ( )No	( )Yes ( )No	( )Yes ( )No	( )Yes ( )No
Aerobic Workout	Aerobic Workout	Aerobic Workout	Aerobic Workout
30 min.	**40 min.**		**70 min.**
60 % = _____bpm	70 % = _____bpm	% = _____bpm	60 % = _____bpm
Body Part Workout	Body Part Workout	Body Part Workout	Body Part Workout
1.____ × ____ sets 2.____ × ____ sets 3.____ × ____ sets 4.____ × ____ sets 5.____ × ____ sets	1.____ × 3 sets 2.____ × 2 sets 3.____ × 2 sets 4.____ × 1 sets 5.____ × 1 sets	1.____ × 1 sets 2.____ × 2 sets 3.____ × 3 sets 4.____ × 2 sets 5.____ × 1 sets	1.____ × 3 sets 2.____ × 3 sets 3.____ × 2 sets 4.____ × 2 sets 5.____ × 1 sets
( )Yes ( )No	( )Yes ( )No	( )Yes ( )No	( )Yes ( )No

My Working Pulse Rate	WEEK 7		
60% = _____ bpm **70%** = _____ bpm **80%** = _____ bpm	**SUNDAY**	**MONDAY**	**TUESDAY**
Resting Pulse Rate	_____ bpm	_____ bpm	_____ bpm
Warm-Up Exercises	( )Yes ( )No	( )Yes ( )No	( )Yes ( )No
Total Scheduled Walking Time (Or Other Aerobic Workout)	Aerobic Workout **REST DAY**	Aerobic Workout	Aerobic Workout **50 min.**
Working Heart Rate	_____ % = _____ bpm	_____ % = _____ bpm	60 % = _____ bpm
Body Parts (Listed By Priority)	Body Part Workout 1._____ × _____ sets 2._____ × _____ sets 3._____ × _____ sets 4._____ × _____ sets 5._____ × _____ sets	Body Part Workout 1._____ × 4 sets 2._____ × 3 sets 3._____ × 2 sets 4._____ × 2 sets 5._____ × 1 sets	Body Part Workout 1._____ × 3 sets 2._____ × 2 sets 3._____ × 2 sets 4._____ × 1 sets 5._____ × 1 sets
Cool-Down Exercises	( )Yes ( )No	( )Yes ( )No	( )Yes ( )No
Notes/Comments On Today's Workout			

A Half Year In Your Life . . .

124

WEDNESDAY	THURSDAY	FRIDAY	SATURDAY
_____ bpm	_____ bpm	_____ bpm	_____ bpm
( )Yes ( )No	( )Yes ( )No	( )Yes ( )No	( )Yes ( )No
Aerobic Workout	**Aerobic Workout**	**Aerobic Workout**	**Aerobic Workout**
30 min.	**45 min.**		**80 min.**
__60__ % = _____ bpm	__70__ % = _____ bpm	_____ % = _____ bpm	__60__ % = _____ bpm
Body Part Workout	**Body Part Workout**	**Body Part Workout**	**Body Part Workout**
1.____ × ____ sets 2.____ × ____ sets 3.____ × ____ sets 4.____ × ____ sets 5.____ × ____ sets	1.____ × 3 sets 2.____ × 2 sets 3.____ × 2 sets 4.____ × 1 sets 5.____ × 1 sets	1.____ × 1 sets 2.____ × 2 sets 3.____ × 3 sets 4.____ × 2 sets 5.____ × 1 sets	1.____ × 2 sets 2.____ × 3 sets 3.____ × 2 sets 4.____ × 3 sets 5.____ × 1 sets
( )Yes ( )No	( )Yes ( )No	( )Yes ( )No	( )Yes ( )No

My Working Pulse Rate	WEEK 8		
60% = _____ bpm **70%** = _____ bpm **80%** = _____ bpm	**SUNDAY**	**MONDAY**	**TUESDAY**
Resting Pulse Rate	_____ bpm	_____ bpm	_____ bpm
Warm-Up Exercises	( )Yes ( )No	( )Yes ( )No	( )Yes ( )No
Total Scheduled Walking Time (Or Other Aerobic Workout)	Aerobic Workout **REST DAY**	Aerobic Workout	Aerobic Workout **45 min.**
Working Heart Rate	_____ % = _____ bpm	_____ % = _____ bpm	_70_ % = _____ bpm
Body Parts (Listed By Priority)	Body Part Workout 1._____ × _____ sets 2._____ × _____ sets 3._____ × _____ sets 4._____ × _____ sets 5._____ × _____ sets	Body Part Workout 1._____ × 3 sets 2._____ × 2 sets 3._____ × 2 sets 4._____ × 1 sets 5._____ × 1 sets	Body Part Workout 1._____ × 2 sets 2._____ × 1 sets 3._____ × 1 sets 4._____ × 1 sets 5._____ × 0 sets
Cool-Down Exercises	( )Yes ( )No	( )Yes ( )No	( )Yes ( )No
Notes/Comments On Today's Workout			

A Half Year In Your Life . . . .

126

WEDNESDAY	THURSDAY	FRIDAY	SATURDAY
_____ bpm	_____ bpm	_____ bpm	_____ bpm
( )Yes ( )No	( )Yes ( )No	( )Yes ( )No	( )Yes ( )No
Aerobic Workout	Aerobic Workout	Aerobic Workout	Aerobic Workout
25 min.	**30 min.**		**60 min.**
_60_ % = _____bpm	_70_ % = _____bpm	___ % = _____bpm	_70_ % = _____bpm
Body Part Workout	Body Part Workout	Body Part Workout	Body Part Workout
1.____ × ____ sets 2.____ × ____ sets 3.____ × ____ sets 4.____ × ____ sets 5.____ × ____ sets	1.____ × 2 sets 2.____ × 2 sets 3.____ × 1 sets 4.____ × 1 sets 5.____ × 1 sets	1.____ × 1 sets 2.____ × 2 sets 3.____ × 3 sets 4.____ × 2 sets 5.____ × 1 sets	1.____ × 2 sets 2.____ × 2 sets 3.____ × 2 sets 4.____ × 1 sets 5.____ × 1 sets
( )Yes ( )No	( )Yes ( )No	( )Yes ( )No	( )Yes ( )No

My Working Pulse Rate	WEEK 9		
$60\% =$ _____ bpm $70\% =$ _____ bpm $80\% =$ _____ bpm	**SUNDAY**	**MONDAY**	**TUESDAY**
Resting Pulse Rate	_____ bpm	_____ bpm	_____ bpm
Warm-Up Exercises	( )Yes ( )No	( )Yes ( )No	( )Yes ( )No
Total Scheduled Walking Time (Or Other Aerobic Workout)	Aerobic Workout **REST DAY**	Aerobic Workout	Aerobic Workout **45 min.**
Working Heart Rate	_____% = _____ bpm	_____% = _____ bpm	_70_ % = _____ bpm
Body Parts (Listed By Priority)	Body Part Workout 1.____ × ____ sets 2.____ × ____ sets 3.____ × ____ sets 4.____ × ____ sets 5.____ × ____ sets	Body Part Workout 1.____ × 3 sets 2.____ × 3 sets 3.____ × 2 sets 4.____ × 2 sets 5.____ × 1 sets	Body Part Workout 1.____ × 2 sets 2.____ × 2 sets 3.____ × 1 sets 4.____ × 1 sets 5.____ × 1 sets
Cool-Down Exercises	( )Yes ( )No	( )Yes ( )No	( )Yes ( )No
Notes/Comments On Today's Workout			

A Half Year In Your Life . . .

WEDNESDAY	THURSDAY	FRIDAY	SATURDAY
_____ bpm	_____ bpm	_____ bpm	_____ bpm
( )Yes ( )No	( )Yes ( )No	( )Yes ( )No	( )Yes ( )No
Aerobic Workout	Aerobic Workout	Aerobic Workout	Aerobic Workout
30 min.	**30 min.**		**60 min.**
_60_ % = _____bpm	_70_ % = _____bpm	_____ % = _____bpm	_70_ % = _____bpm
Body Part Workout	Body Part Workout	Body Part Workout	Body Part Workout
1.____ × ____ sets 2.____ × ____ sets 3.____ × ____ sets 4.____ × ____ sets 5.____ × ____ sets	1.____ × 2 sets 2.____ × 2 sets 3.____ × 2 sets 4.____ × 1 sets 5.____ × 1 sets	1.____ × 1 sets 2.____ × 2 sets 3.____ × 3 sets 4.____ × 2 sets 5.____ × 1 sets	1.____ × 3 sets 2.____ × 3 sets 3.____ × 2 sets 4.____ × 2 sets 5.____ × 1 sets
( )Yes ( )No	( )Yes ( )No	( )Yes ( )No	( )Yes ( )No

My Working Pulse Rate	WEEK 10		
60% = _____ bpm **70%** = _____ bpm **80%** = _____ bpm	**SUNDAY**	**MONDAY**	**TUESDAY**
Resting Pulse Rate	_____ bpm	_____ bpm	_____ bpm
Warm-Up Exercises	( )Yes ( )No	( )Yes ( )No	( )Yes ( )No
Total Scheduled Walking Time (Or Other Aerobic Workout)	Aerobic Workout **REST DAY**	Aerobic Workout	Aerobic Workout **45 min.**
Working Heart Rate	_____ % = _____ bpm	_____ % = _____ bpm	_70_ % = _____ bpm
Body Parts (Listed By Priority)	Body Part Workout 1._____ × _____ sets 2._____ × _____ sets 3._____ × _____ sets 4._____ × _____ sets 5._____ × _____ sets	Body Part Workout 1._____ × 4 sets 2._____ × 3 sets 3._____ × 2 sets 4._____ × 2 sets 5._____ × 1 sets	Body Part Workout 1._____ × 3 sets 2._____ × 2 sets 3._____ × 1 sets 4._____ × 1 sets 5._____ × 0 sets
Cool-Down Exercises	( )Yes ( )No	( )Yes ( )No	( )Yes ( )No
Notes/Comments On Today's Workout			

A Half Year In Your Life . . . .

WEDNESDAY	THURSDAY	FRIDAY	SATURDAY
_____ bpm	_____ bpm	_____ bpm	_____ bpm
( )Yes ( )No	( )Yes ( )No	( )Yes ( )No	( )Yes ( )No
Aerobic Workout	Aerobic Workout	Aerobic Workout	Aerobic Workout
30 min.	**40 min.**		**70 min.**
_60_ % = _____ bpm	_70_ % = _____ bpm	_____ % = _____ bpm	_60_ % = _____ bpm
Body Part Workout	Body Part Workout	Body Part Workout	Body Part Workout
1._____ × _____ sets 2._____ × _____ sets 3._____ × _____ sets 4._____ × _____ sets 5._____ × _____ sets	1._____ × 3 sets 2._____ × 2 sets 3._____ × 2 sets 4._____ × 1 sets 5._____ × 1 sets	1._____ × 1 sets 2._____ × 2 sets 3._____ × 3 sets 4._____ × 2 sets 5._____ × 1 sets	1._____ × 3 sets 2._____ × 3 sets 3._____ × 2 sets 4._____ × 2 sets 5._____ × 1 sets
( )Yes ( )No	( )Yes ( )No	( )Yes ( )No	( )Yes ( )No

My Working Pulse Rate	**WEEK 11**		
60% = _____ bpm **70%** = _____ bpm **80%** = _____ bpm	**SUNDAY**	**MONDAY**	**TUESDAY**
Resting Pulse Rate	_____ bpm	_____ bpm	_____ bpm
Warm-Up Exercises	( )Yes ( )No	( )Yes ( )No	( )Yes ( )No
Total Scheduled Walking Time (Or Other Aerobic Workout)	Aerobic Workout **REST DAY**	Aerobic Workout	Aerobic Workout **50 min.**
Working Heart Rate	_____ % = _____ bpm	_____ % = _____ bpm	60 % = _____ bpm
Body Parts (Listed By Priority)	Body Part Workout 1._____ × _____ sets 2._____ × _____ sets 3._____ × _____ sets 4._____ × _____ sets 5._____ × _____ sets	Body Part Workout 1._____ × 4 sets 2._____ × 3 sets 3._____ × 2 sets 4._____ × 2 sets 5._____ × 1 sets	Body Part Workout 1._____ × 3 sets 2._____ × 2 sets 3._____ × 2 sets 4._____ × 1 sets 5._____ × 1 sets
Cool-Down Exercises	( )Yes ( )No	( )Yes ( )No	( )Yes ( )No
Notes/Comments On Today's Workout			

A Half Year In Your Life . . .

WEDNESDAY	THURSDAY	FRIDAY	SATURDAY
_____ bpm	_____ bpm	_____ bpm	_____ bpm
( )Yes ( )No	( )Yes ( )No	( )Yes ( )No	( )Yes ( )No
Aerobic Workout	Aerobic Workout	Aerobic Workout	Aerobic Workout
30 min.	45 min.		80 min.
__60__ % = _____ bpm	__70__ % = _____ bpm	_____ % = _____ bpm	__60__ % = _____ bpm
Body Part Workout	Body Part Workout	Body Part Workout	Body Part Workout
1._____ × _____ sets 2._____ × _____ sets 3._____ × _____ sets 4._____ × _____ sets 5._____ × _____ sets	1._____ × 3 sets 2._____ × 2 sets 3._____ × 2 sets 4._____ × 1 sets 5._____ × 1 sets	1._____ × 1 sets 2._____ × 2 sets 3._____ × 3 sets 4._____ × 2 sets 5._____ × 1 sets	1._____ × 2 sets 2._____ × 3 sets 3._____ × 2 sets 4._____ × 3 sets 5._____ × 1 sets
( )Yes ( )No	( )Yes ( )No	( )Yes ( )No	( )Yes ( )No

My Working Pulse Rate			
60% = _____ bpm 70% = _____ bpm 80% = _____ bpm	**SUNDAY**	**MONDAY**	**TUESDAY**
Resting Pulse Rate	_____ bpm	_____ bpm	_____ bpm
Warm-Up Exercises	( )Yes ( )No	( )Yes ( )No	( )Yes ( )No
Total Scheduled Walking Time (Or Other Aerobic Workout)	Aerobic Workout **REST DAY**	Aerobic Workout	Aerobic Workout **45 min.**
Working Heart Rate	_____ % = _____ bpm	_____ % = _____ bpm	70 % = _____ bpm
Body Parts (Listed By Priority)	Body Part Workout 1. _____ × _____ sets 2. _____ × _____ sets 3. _____ × _____ sets 4. _____ × _____ sets 5. _____ × _____ sets	Body Part Workout 1. _____ × 3 sets 2. _____ × 3 sets 3. _____ × 2 sets 4. _____ × 2 sets 5. _____ × 1 sets	Body Part Workout 1. _____ × 2 sets 2. _____ × 2 sets 3. _____ × 1 sets 4. _____ × 1 sets 5. _____ × 1 sets
Cool-Down Exercises	( )Yes ( )No	( )Yes ( )No	( )Yes ( )No
Notes/Comments On Today's Workout			

A Half Year In Your Life . . .

WEDNESDAY	THURSDAY	FRIDAY	SATURDAY
_____ bpm	_____ bpm	_____ bpm	_____ bpm
( )Yes ( )No	( )Yes ( )No	( )Yes ( )No	( )Yes ( )No
Aerobic Workout	Aerobic Workout	Aerobic Workout	Aerobic Workout
30 min.	**30 min.**		**60 min.**
__60__ % = _____ bpm	__70__ % = _____ bpm	_____ % = _____ bpm	__70__ % = _____ bpm
Body Part Workout	Body Part Workout	Body Part Workout	Body Part Workout
1._____ × _____ sets 2._____ × _____ sets 3._____ × _____ sets 4._____ × _____ sets 5._____ × _____ sets	1._____ × 2 sets 2._____ × 2 sets 3._____ × 2 sets 4._____ × 1 sets 5._____ × 1 sets	1._____ × 1 sets 2._____ × 2 sets 3._____ × 3 sets 4._____ × 2 sets 5._____ × 1 sets	1._____ × 3 sets 2._____ × 3 sets 3._____ × 2 sets 4._____ × 2 sets 5._____ × 1 sets
( )Yes ( )No	( )Yes ( )No	( )Yes ( )No	( )Yes ( )No

My Working Pulse Rate	SUNDAY	MONDAY	TUESDAY
60% = _____ bpm 70% = _____ bpm 80% = _____ bpm			
Resting Pulse Rate	_____ bpm	_____ bpm	_____ bpm
Warm-Up Exercises	( )Yes ( )No	( )Yes ( )No	( )Yes ( )No
Total Scheduled Walking Time (Or Other Aerobic Workout)	Aerobic Workout **REST DAY**	Aerobic Workout 	Aerobic Workout **45 min.**
Working Heart Rate	_____ % = _____ bpm	_____ % = _____ bpm	70 % = _____ bpm
Body Parts (Listed By Priority)	Body Part Workout 1.____ × ____ sets 2.____ × ____ sets 3.____ × ____ sets 4.____ × ____ sets 5.____ × ____ sets	Body Part Workout 1.____ × 4 sets 2.____ × 3 sets 3.____ × 2 sets 4.____ × 2 sets 5.____ × 1 sets	Body Part Workout 1.____ × 3 sets 2.____ × 2 sets 3.____ × 1 sets 4.____ × 1 sets 5.____ × 0 sets
Cool-Down Exercises	( )Yes ( )No	( )Yes ( )No	( )Yes ( )No
Notes/Comments On Today's Workout			

A Half Year In Your Life . . .

WEDNESDAY	THURSDAY	FRIDAY	SATURDAY
_____ bpm	_____ bpm	_____ bpm	_____ bpm
( )Yes ( )No	( )Yes ( )No	( )Yes ( )No	( )Yes ( )No
Aerobic Workout	Aerobic Workout	Aerobic Workout	Aerobic Workout
30 min.	40 min.		70 min.
60 % = _____ bpm	70 % = _____ bpm	___ % = _____ bpm	60 % = _____ bpm
Body Part Workout	Body Part Workout	Body Part Workout	Body Part Workout
1.____ × ____ sets 2.____ × ____ sets 3.____ × ____ sets 4.____ × ____ sets 5.____ × ____ sets	1.____ × 3 sets 2.____ × 2 sets 3.____ × 2 sets 4.____ × 1 sets 5.____ × 1 sets	1.____ × 1 sets 2.____ × 2 sets 3.____ × 3 sets 4.____ × 2 sets 5.____ × 1 sets	1.____ × 3 sets 2.____ × 3 sets 3.____ × 2 sets 4.____ × 2 sets 5.____ × 1 sets
( )Yes ( )No	( )Yes ( )No	( )Yes ( )No	( )Yes ( )No

My Working Pulse Rate	WEEK 14		
60% = _____ bpm 70% = _____ bpm 80% = _____ bpm	**SUNDAY**	**MONDAY**	**TUESDAY**
Resting Pulse Rate	_____ bpm	_____ bpm	_____ bpm
Warm-Up Exercises	( )Yes ( )No	( )Yes ( )No	( )Yes ( )No
Total Scheduled Walking Time (Or Other Aerobic Workout)	Aerobic Workout **REST DAY**	Aerobic Workout 	Aerobic Workout **50 min.**
Working Heart Rate	_____ % = _____ bpm	_____ % = _____ bpm	60 % = _____ bpm
Body Parts (Listed By Priority)	Body Part Workout 1. _____ × _____ sets 2. _____ × _____ sets 3. _____ × _____ sets 4. _____ × _____ sets 5. _____ × _____ sets	Body Part Workout 1. _____ × 4 sets 2. _____ × 3 sets 3. _____ × 2 sets 4. _____ × 2 sets 5. _____ × 1 sets	Body Part Workout 1. _____ × 3 sets 2. _____ × 2 sets 3. _____ × 2 sets 4. _____ × 1 sets 5. _____ × 1 sets
Cool-Down Exercises	( )Yes ( )No	( )Yes ( )No	( )Yes ( )No
Notes/Comments On Today's Workout			

A Half Year In Your Life . . .

138

WEDNESDAY	THURSDAY	FRIDAY	SATURDAY
_____ bpm	_____ bpm	_____ bpm	_____ bpm
( )Yes ( )No	( )Yes ( )No	( )Yes ( )No	( )Yes ( )No
Aerobic Workout	Aerobic Workout	Aerobic Workout	Aerobic Workout
30 min.	**45 min.**		**80 min.**
__60__ % = _____ bpm	__70__ % = _____ bpm	_____ % = _____ bpm	__60__ % = _____ bpm
Body Part Workout	Body Part Workout	Body Part Workout	Body Part Workout
1._____ × _____ sets 2._____ × _____ sets 3._____ × _____ sets 4._____ × _____ sets 5._____ × _____ sets	1._____ × 3 sets 2._____ × 2 sets 3._____ × 2 sets 4._____ × 1 sets 5._____ × 1 sets	1._____ × 1 sets 2._____ × 2 sets 3._____ × 3 sets 4._____ × 2 sets 5._____ × 1 sets	1._____ × 2 sets 2._____ × 3 sets 3._____ × 2 sets 4._____ × 3 sets 5._____ × 1 sets
( )Yes ( )No	( )Yes ( )No	( )Yes ( )No	( )Yes ( )No

A Half Year In Your Life . . .

My Working Pulse Rate			
60% = _____ bpm 70% = _____ bpm 80% = _____ bpm	**WEEK 15**		
	SUNDAY	**MONDAY**	**TUESDAY**
Resting Pulse Rate	_____ bpm	_____ bpm	_____ bpm
Warm-Up Exercises	( )Yes ( )No	( )Yes ( )No	( )Yes ( )No
Total Scheduled Walking Time (Or Other Aerobic Workout)	Aerobic Workout **REST DAY**	Aerobic Workout	Aerobic Workout **60 min.**
Working Heart Rate	_____ % = _____ bpm	_____ % = _____ bpm	60 % = _____ bpm
Body Parts (Listed By Priority)	Body Part Workout 1._____ × _____ sets 2._____ × _____ sets 3._____ × _____ sets 4._____ × _____ sets 5._____ × _____ sets	Body Part Workout 1._____ × 4 sets 2._____ × 2 sets 3._____ × 3 sets 4._____ × 2 sets 5._____ × 1 sets	Body Part Workout 1._____ × 2 sets 2._____ × 2 sets 3._____ × 1 sets 4._____ × 1 sets 5._____ × 1 sets
Cool-Down Exercises	( )Yes ( )No	( )Yes ( )No	( )Yes ( )No
Notes/Comments On Today's Workout			

WEDNESDAY	THURSDAY	FRIDAY	SATURDAY
_____ bpm	_____ bpm	_____ bpm	_____ bpm
( )Yes ( )No	( )Yes ( )No	( )Yes ( )No	( )Yes ( )No
Aerobic Workout	**Aerobic Workout**	**Aerobic Workout**	**Aerobic Workout**
30 min.	**50 min.**		**90 min.**
60 % = _____ bpm	70 % = _____ bpm	____ % = _____ bpm	60 % = _____ bpm
Body Part Workout	**Body Part Workout**	**Body Part Workout**	**Body Part Workout**
1._____ × _____ sets 2._____ × _____ sets 3._____ × _____ sets 4._____ × _____ sets 5._____ × _____ sets	1._____ × 3 sets 2._____ × 2 sets 3._____ × 3 sets 4._____ × 1 sets 5._____ × 1 sets	1._____ × 1 sets 2._____ × 2 sets 3._____ × 3 sets 4._____ × 2 sets 5._____ × 1 sets	1._____ × 2 sets 2._____ × 2 sets 3._____ × 1 sets 4._____ × 1 sets 5._____ × 1 sets
( )Yes ( )No	( )Yes ( )No	( )Yes ( )No	( )Yes ( )No

My Working Pulse Rate	WEEK 16		
60% = _____ bpm **70%** = _____ bpm **80%** = _____ bpm	**SUNDAY**	**MONDAY**	**TUESDAY**
Resting Pulse Rate	_____ bpm	_____ bpm	_____ bpm
Warm-Up Exercises	( )Yes ( )No	( )Yes ( )No	( )Yes ( )No
Total Scheduled Walking Time (Or Other Aerobic Workout)	Aerobic Workout **REST DAY**	Aerobic Workout	Aerobic Workout **45 min.**
Working Heart Rate	_____ % = _____ bpm	_____ % = _____ bpm	70 % = _____ bpm
Body Parts (Listed By Priority)	Body Part Workout 1._____ × _____ sets 2._____ × _____ sets 3._____ × _____ sets 4._____ × _____ sets 5._____ × _____ sets	Body Part Workout 1._____ × 3 sets 2._____ × 3 sets 3._____ × 2 sets 4._____ × 2 sets 5._____ × 1 sets	Body Part Workout 1._____ × 2 sets 2._____ × 2 sets 3._____ × 1 sets 4._____ × 1 sets 5._____ × 1 sets
Cool-Down Exercises	( )Yes ( )No	( )Yes ( )No	( )Yes ( )No
Notes/Comments On Today's Workout			

A Half Year In Your Life . . . .

WEDNESDAY	THURSDAY	FRIDAY	SATURDAY
_____ bpm	_____ bpm	_____ bpm	_____ bpm
( )Yes ( )No	( )Yes ( )No	( )Yes ( )No	( )Yes ( )No
Aerobic Workout	Aerobic Workout	Aerobic Workout	Aerobic Workout
30 min.	**30 min.**		**60 min.**
__60__ % = _____bpm	__70__ % = _____bpm	___ % = _____bpm	__70__ % = _____bpm
Body Part Workout	Body Part Workout	Body Part Workout	Body Part Workout
1._____ × _____ sets 2._____ × _____ sets 3._____ × _____ sets 4._____ × _____ sets 5._____ × _____ sets	1._____ × 2 sets 2._____ × 2 sets 3._____ × 2 sets 4._____ × 1 sets 5._____ × 1 sets	1._____ × 1 sets 2._____ × 2 sets 3._____ × 3 sets 4._____ × 2 sets 5._____ × 1 sets	1._____ × 3 sets 2._____ × 3 sets 3._____ × 2 sets 4._____ × 2 sets 5._____ × 1 sets
( )Yes ( )No	( )Yes ( )No	( )Yes ( )No	( )Yes ( )No

My Working Pulse Rate			
60% = _____ bpm **70%** = _____ bpm **80%** = _____ bpm	**WEEK 17**		
	SUNDAY	**MONDAY**	**TUESDAY**
Resting Pulse Rate	_____ bpm	_____ bpm	_____ bpm
Warm-Up Exercises	( )Yes ( )No	( )Yes ( )No	( )Yes ( )No
Total Scheduled Walking Time (Or Other Aerobic Workout)	Aerobic Workout **REST DAY**	Aerobic Workout	Aerobic Workout **45 min.**
Working Heart Rate	_____% = _____ bpm	_____% = _____ bpm	70 % = _____ bpm
Body Parts (Listed By Priority)	Body Part Workout 1._____ × _____ sets 2._____ × _____ sets 3._____ × _____ sets 4._____ × _____ sets 5._____ × _____ sets	Body Part Workout 1._____ × 4 sets 2._____ × 3 sets 3._____ × 2 sets 4._____ × 2 sets 5._____ × 1 sets	Body Part Workout 1._____ × 3 sets 2._____ × 2 sets 3._____ × 1 sets 4._____ × 1 sets 5._____ × 0 sets
Cool-Down Exercises	( )Yes ( )No	( )Yes ( )No	( )Yes ( )No
Notes/Comments On Today's Workout			

A Half Year In Your Life . . . .

WEDNESDAY	THURSDAY	FRIDAY	SATURDAY
_____ bpm	_____ bpm	_____ bpm	_____ bpm
( )Yes ( )No	( )Yes ( )No	( )Yes ( )No	( )Yes ( )No
Aerobic Workout	Aerobic Workout	Aerobic Workout	Aerobic Workout
30 min.	40 min.		70 min.
_60_ % = _____ bpm	_70_ % = _____ bpm	____ % = _____ bpm	_60_ % = _____ bpm
Body Part Workout	Body Part Workout	Body Part Workout	Body Part Workout
1.____ × ____ sets 2.____ × ____ sets 3.____ × ____ sets 4.____ × ____ sets 5.____ × ____ sets	1.____ × 3 sets 2.____ × 2 sets 3.____ × 2 sets 4.____ × 1 sets 5.____ × 1 sets	1.____ × 1 sets 2.____ × 2 sets 3.____ × 3 sets 4.____ × 2 sets 5.____ × 1 sets	1.____ × 3 sets 2.____ × 3 sets 3.____ × 2 sets 4.____ × 2 sets 5.____ × 1 sets
( )Yes ( )No	( )Yes ( )No	( )Yes ( )No	( )Yes ( )No

My Working Pulse Rate	WEEK 18		
60% = _____ bpm 70% = _____ bpm 80% = _____ bpm	SUNDAY	MONDAY	TUESDAY
Resting Pulse Rate	_____ bpm	_____ bpm	_____ bpm
Warm-Up Exercises	( )Yes ( )No	( )Yes ( )No	( )Yes ( )No
Total Scheduled Walking Time (Or Other Aerobic Workout)	Aerobic Workout **REST DAY**	Aerobic Workout	Aerobic Workout **50 min.**
Working Heart Rate	_____% = _____bpm	_____% = _____bpm	60 % = _____bpm
Body Parts (Listed By Priority)	Body Part Workout 1._____ × _____ sets 2._____ × _____ sets 3._____ × _____ sets 4._____ × _____ sets 5._____ × _____ sets	Body Part Workout 1._____ × 4 sets 2._____ × 3 sets 3._____ × 2 sets 4._____ × 2 sets 5._____ × 1 sets	Body Part Workout 1._____ × 3 sets 2._____ × 2 sets 3._____ × 2 sets 4._____ × 1 sets 5._____ × 1 sets
Cool-Down Exercises	( )Yes ( )No	( )Yes ( )No	( )Yes ( )No
Notes/Comments On Today's Workout			

A Half Year In Your Life . . .

WEDNESDAY	THURSDAY	FRIDAY	SATURDAY
_____ bpm	_____ bpm	_____ bpm	_____ bpm
( )Yes ( )No	( )Yes ( )No	( )Yes ( )No	( )Yes ( )No
Aerobic Workout	Aerobic Workout	Aerobic Workout	Aerobic Workout
30 min.	**45 min.**		**80 min.**
__60__ % = _____ bpm	__70__ % = _____ bpm	_____ % = _____ bpm	__60__ % = _____ bpm
Body Part Workout	Body Part Workout	Body Part Workout	Body Part Workout
1._____ × _____ sets 2._____ × _____ sets 3._____ × _____ sets 4._____ × _____ sets 5._____ × _____ sets	1._____ × 3 sets 2._____ × 2 sets 3._____ × 2 sets 4._____ × 1 sets 5._____ × 1 sets	1._____ × 1 sets 2._____ × 2 sets 3._____ × 3 sets 4._____ × 2 sets 5._____ × 1 sets	1._____ × 2 sets 2._____ × 3 sets 3._____ × 2 sets 4._____ × 3 sets 5._____ × 1 sets
( )Yes ( )No	( )Yes ( )No	( )Yes ( )No	( )Yes ( )No

My Working Pulse Rate			
60% = _____ bpm 70% = _____ bpm 80% = _____ bpm	**WEEK 19**		
	SUNDAY	**MONDAY**	**TUESDAY**
Resting Pulse Rate	_____ bpm	_____ bpm	_____ bpm
Warm-Up Exercises	( )Yes ( )No	( )Yes ( )No	( )Yes ( )No
Total Scheduled Walking Time (Or Other Aerobic Workout)	Aerobic Workout **REST DAY**	Aerobic Workout	Aerobic Workout **60 min.**
Working Heart Rate	_____ % = _____ bpm	_____ % = _____ bpm	60 % = _____ bpm
Body Parts (Listed By Priority)	Body Part Workout 1._____ × _____ sets 2._____ × _____ sets 3._____ × _____ sets 4._____ × _____ sets 5._____ × _____ sets	Body Part Workout 1._____ × 4 sets 2._____ × 2 sets 3._____ × 3 sets 4._____ × 2 sets 5._____ × 1 sets	Body Part Workout 1._____ × 2 sets 2._____ × 2 sets 3._____ × 1 sets 4._____ × 1 sets 5._____ × 1 sets
Cool-Down Exercises	( )Yes ( )No	( )Yes ( )No	( )Yes ( )No
Notes/Comments On Today's Workout			

A Half Year In Your Life . . .

148

WEDNESDAY	THURSDAY	FRIDAY	SATURDAY
_____ bpm	_____ bpm	_____ bpm	_____ bpm
( )Yes ( )No	( )Yes ( )No	( )Yes ( )No	( )Yes ( )No
Aerobic Workout	Aerobic Workout	Aerobic Workout	Aerobic Workout
30 min.	50 min.		90 min.
60 % = _____ bpm	70 % = _____ bpm	___ % = _____ bpm	60 % = _____ bpm
Body Part Workout	Body Part Workout	Body Part Workout	Body Part Workout
1._____ × _____ sets 2._____ × _____ sets 3._____ × _____ sets 4._____ × _____ sets 5._____ × _____ sets	1._____ × 3 sets 2._____ × 2 sets 3._____ × 3 sets 4._____ × 1 sets 5._____ × 1 sets	1._____ × 1 sets 2._____ × 2 sets 3._____ × 3 sets 4._____ × 2 sets 5._____ × 1 sets	1._____ × 2 sets 2._____ × 2 sets 3._____ × 1 sets 4._____ × 1 sets 5._____ × 1 sets
( )Yes ( )No	( )Yes ( )No	( )Yes ( )No	( )Yes ( )No

A Half Year In Your Life . . . .

WEEK 20

My Working Pulse Rate	SUNDAY	MONDAY	TUESDAY
60% = _____ bpm 70% = _____ bpm 80% = _____ bpm			
Resting Pulse Rate	_____ bpm	_____ bpm	_____ bpm
Warm-Up Exercises	( )Yes ( )No	( )Yes ( )No	( )Yes ( )No
Total Scheduled Walking Time (Or Other Aerobic Workout)	Aerobic Workout **REST DAY**	Aerobic Workout	Aerobic Workout **45 min.**
Working Heart Rate	_____ % = _____ bpm	_____ % = _____ bpm	70 % = _____ bpm
Body Parts (Listed By Priority)	Body Part Workout 1._____ × _____ sets 2._____ × _____ sets 3._____ × _____ sets 4._____ × _____ sets 5._____ × _____ sets	Body Part Workout 1._____ × 4 sets 2._____ × 3 sets 3._____ × 2 sets 4._____ × 2 sets 5._____ × 1 sets	Body Part Workout 1._____ × 3 sets 2._____ × 2 sets 3._____ × 1 sets 4._____ × 1 sets 5._____ × 0 sets
Cool-Down Exercises	( )Yes ( )No	( )Yes ( )No	( )Yes ( )No
Notes/Comments On Today's Workout			

WEDNESDAY	THURSDAY	FRIDAY	SATURDAY
_____ bpm	_____ bpm	_____ bpm	_____ bpm
( )Yes ( )No	( )Yes ( )No	( )Yes ( )No	( )Yes ( )No
Aerobic Workout	Aerobic Workout	Aerobic Workout	Aerobic Workout
30 min.	**40 min.**		**70 min.**
_60_ % = _____ bpm	_70_ % = _____ bpm	_____ % = _____ bpm	_60_ % = _____ bpm
Body Part Workout	Body Part Workout	Body Part Workout	Body Part Workout
1._____ × _____ sets 2._____ × _____ sets 3._____ × _____ sets 4._____ × _____ sets 5._____ × _____ sets	1._____ × 3 sets 2._____ × 2 sets 3._____ × 2 sets 4._____ × 1 sets 5._____ × 1 sets	1._____ × 1 sets 2._____ × 2 sets 3._____ × 3 sets 4._____ × 2 sets 5._____ × 1 sets	1._____ × 3 sets 2._____ × 3 sets 3._____ × 2 sets 4._____ × 2 sets 5._____ × 1 sets
( )Yes ( )No	( )Yes ( )No	( )Yes ( )No	( )Yes ( )No

My Working Pulse Rate	**WEEK 21**		
60% = _____ bpm **70%** = _____ bpm **80%** = _____ bpm	**SUNDAY**	**MONDAY**	**TUESDAY**
Resting Pulse Rate	_____ bpm	_____ bpm	_____ bpm
Warm-Up Exercises	( )Yes ( )No	( )Yes ( )No	( )Yes ( )No
Total Scheduled Walking Time (Or Other Aerobic Workout)	Aerobic Workout **REST DAY**	Aerobic Workout	Aerobic Workout **50 min.**
Working Heart Rate	_____ % = _____ bpm	_____ % = _____ bpm	60 % = _____ bpm
Body Parts (Listed By Priority)	Body Part Workout 1._____ × _____ sets 2._____ × _____ sets 3._____ × _____ sets 4._____ × _____ sets 5._____ × _____ sets	Body Part Workout 1._____ × 4 sets 2._____ × 3 sets 3._____ × 2 sets 4._____ × 2 sets 5._____ × 1 sets	Body Part Workout 1._____ × 3 sets 2._____ × 2 sets 3._____ × 2 sets 4._____ × 1 sets 5._____ × 1 sets
Cool-Down Exercises	( )Yes ( )No	( )Yes ( )No	( )Yes ( )No
Notes/Comments On Today's Workout			

A Half Year In Your Life . . .

WEDNESDAY	THURSDAY	FRIDAY	SATURDAY
_____ bpm	_____ bpm	_____ bpm	_____ bpm
( )Yes ( )No	( )Yes ( )No	( )Yes ( )No	( )Yes ( )No
Aerobic Workout	Aerobic Workout	Aerobic Workout	Aerobic Workout
30 min.	45 min.		80 min.
60 % = _____ bpm	70 % = _____ bpm	___ % = _____ bpm	60 % = _____ bpm
Body Part Workout	Body Part Workout	Body Part Workout	Body Part Workout
1._____ × _____ sets 2._____ × _____ sets 3._____ × _____ sets 4._____ × _____ sets 5._____ × _____ sets	1._____ × 3 sets 2._____ × 2 sets 3._____ × 2 sets 4._____ × 1 sets 5._____ × 1 sets	1._____ × 1 sets 2._____ × 2 sets 3._____ × 3 sets 4._____ × 2 sets 5._____ × 1 sets	1._____ × 2 sets 2._____ × 3 sets 3._____ × 2 sets 4._____ × 3 sets 5._____ × 1 sets
( )Yes ( )No	( )Yes ( )No	( )Yes ( )No	( )Yes ( )No

WEEK 22

My Working Pulse Rate	SUNDAY	MONDAY	TUESDAY
60% = _____ bpm 70% = _____ bpm 80% = _____ bpm			
Resting Pulse Rate	_____ bpm	_____ bpm	_____ bpm
Warm-Up Exercises	( )Yes ( )No	( )Yes ( )No	( )Yes ( )No
Total Scheduled Walking Time (Or Other Aerobic Workout)	Aerobic Workout **REST DAY**	Aerobic Workout	Aerobic Workout **60 min.**
Working Heart Rate	_____ % = _____ bpm	_____ % = _____ bpm	60 % = _____ bpm
Body Parts (Listed By Priority)	Body Part Workout 1._____ × _____ sets 2._____ × _____ sets 3._____ × _____ sets 4._____ × _____ sets 5._____ × _____ sets	Body Part Workout 1._____ × 4 sets 2._____ × 2 sets 3._____ × 3 sets 4._____ × 2 sets 5._____ × 1 sets	Body Part Workout 1._____ × 2 sets 2._____ × 2 sets 3._____ × 1 sets 4._____ × 1 sets 5._____ × 1 sets
Cool-Down Exercises	( )Yes ( )No	( )Yes ( )No	( )Yes ( )No
Notes/Comments On Today's Workout			

A Half Year In Your Life . . . . .

WEDNESDAY	THURSDAY	FRIDAY	SATURDAY
_____ bpm	_____ bpm	_____ bpm	_____ bpm
( ) Yes ( ) No	( ) Yes ( ) No	( ) Yes ( ) No	( ) Yes ( ) No
Aerobic Workout	Aerobic Workout	Aerobic Workout	Aerobic Workout
30 min.	**50 min.**		**90 min.**
60 % = _____ bpm	70 % = _____ bpm	___ % = _____ bpm	60 % = _____ bpm
Body Part Workout	Body Part Workout	Body Part Workout	Body Part Workout
1._____ × _____ sets 2._____ × _____ sets 3._____ × _____ sets 4._____ × _____ sets 5._____ × _____ sets	1._____ × 3 sets 2._____ × 2 sets 3._____ × 3 sets 4._____ × 1 sets 5._____ × 1 sets	1._____ × 1 sets 2._____ × 2 sets 3._____ × 3 sets 4._____ × 2 sets 5._____ × 1 sets	1._____ × 2 sets 2._____ × 2 sets 3._____ × 1 sets 4._____ × 1 sets 5._____ × 1 sets
( ) Yes ( ) No	( ) Yes ( ) No	( ) Yes ( ) No	( ) Yes ( ) No

My Working Pulse Rate	WEEK 23		
60% = _____ bpm 70% = _____ bpm 80% = _____ bpm	**SUNDAY**	**MONDAY**	**TUESDAY**
Resting Pulse Rate	_____ bpm	_____ bpm	_____ bpm
Warm-Up Exercises	( )Yes ( )No	( )Yes ( )No	( )Yes ( )No
Total Scheduled Walking Time (Or Other Aerobic Workout)	Aerobic Workout **REST DAY**	Aerobic Workout	Aerobic Workout **60 min.**
Working Heart Rate	_____ % = _____ bpm	_____ % = _____ bpm	_70_ % = _____ bpm
Body Parts (Listed By Priority)	Body Part Workout 1._____ × _____ sets 2._____ × _____ sets 3._____ × _____ sets 4._____ × _____ sets 5._____ × _____ sets	Body Part Workout 1._____ × 4 sets 2._____ × 3 sets 3._____ × 3 sets 4._____ × 2 sets 5._____ × 2 sets	Body Part Workout 1._____ × 2 sets 2._____ × 2 sets 3._____ × 1 sets 4._____ × 2 sets 5._____ × 1 sets
Cool-Down Exercises	( )Yes ( )No	( )Yes ( )No	( )Yes ( )No
Notes/Comments On Today's Workout			

A Half Year In Your Life . . .

WEDNESDAY	THURSDAY	FRIDAY	SATURDAY
_____ bpm	_____ bpm	_____ bpm	_____ bpm
( )Yes ( )No	( )Yes ( )No	( )Yes ( )No	( )Yes ( )No
Aerobic Workout	Aerobic Workout	Aerobic Workout	Aerobic Workout
30 min.	50 min.		90 min.
__60__ % = _____bpm	__70__ % = _____bpm	_____ % = _____bpm	__70__ % = _____bpm
Body Part Workout	Body Part Workout	Body Part Workout	Body Part Workout
1._____ × _____ sets 2._____ × _____ sets 3._____ × _____ sets 4._____ × _____ sets 5._____ × _____ sets	1._____ × 3 sets 2._____ × 3 sets 3._____ × 2 sets 4._____ × 2 sets 5._____ × 1 sets	1._____ × 1 sets 2._____ × 2 sets 3._____ × 3 sets 4._____ × 2 sets 5._____ × 1 sets	1._____ × 2 sets 2._____ × 2 sets 3._____ × 2 sets 4._____ × 1 sets 5._____ × 1 sets
( )Yes ( )No	( )Yes ( )No	( )Yes ( )No	( )Yes ( )No

My Working Pulse Rate	WEEK 24		
60% = _____ bpm 70% = _____ bpm 80% = _____ bpm	**SUNDAY**	**MONDAY**	**TUESDAY**
Resting Pulse Rate	_____ bpm	_____ bpm	_____ bpm
Warm-Up Exercises	( )Yes ( )No	( )Yes ( )No	( )Yes ( )No
Total Scheduled Walking Time (Or Other Aerobic Workout)	Aerobic Workout **REST DAY**	Aerobic Workout	Aerobic Workout **45 min.**
Working Heart Rate	_____ % = _____ bpm	_____ % = _____ bpm	_70_ % = _____ bpm
Body Parts (Listed By Priority)	Body Part Workout 1._____ × _____ sets 2._____ × _____ sets 3._____ × _____ sets 4._____ × _____ sets 5._____ × _____ sets	Body Part Workout 1._____ × 4 sets 2._____ × 3 sets 3._____ × 2 sets 4._____ × 2 sets 5._____ × 1 sets	Body Part Workout 1._____ × 3 sets 2._____ × 2 sets 3._____ × 1 sets 4._____ × 1 sets 5._____ × 0 sets
Cool-Down Exercises	( )Yes ( )No	( )Yes ( )No	( )Yes ( )No
Notes/Comments On Today's Workout			

A Half Year In Your Life . . .

WEDNESDAY	THURSDAY	FRIDAY	SATURDAY
_____ bpm	_____ bpm	_____ bpm	_____ bpm
( )Yes ( )No	( )Yes ( )No	( )Yes ( )No	( )Yes ( )No
Aerobic Workout	Aerobic Workout	Aerobic Workout	Aerobic Workout
30 min.	40 min.		70 min.
60 % = _____ bpm	70 % = _____ bpm	% = _____ bpm	60 % = _____ bpm
Body Part Workout	Body Part Workout	Body Part Workout	Body Part Workout
1._____ × _____ sets 2._____ × _____ sets 3._____ × _____ sets 4._____ × _____ sets 5._____ × _____ sets	1._____ × 3 sets 2._____ × 2 sets 3._____ × 2 sets 4._____ × 1 sets 5._____ × 1 sets	1._____ × 1 sets 2._____ × 2 sets 3._____ × 3 sets 4._____ × 2 sets 5._____ × 1 sets	1._____ × 3 sets 2._____ × 3 sets 3._____ × 2 sets 4._____ × 2 sets 5._____ × 1 sets
( )Yes ( )No	( )Yes ( )No	( )Yes ( )No	( )Yes ( )No

A Half Year In Your Life . . . .

My Working Pulse Rate

60% = _____ bpm
70% = _____ bpm
80% = _____ bpm

WEEK 25

	SUNDAY	MONDAY	TUESDAY
Resting Pulse Rate	_____ bpm	_____ bpm	_____ bpm
Warm-Up Exercises	( )Yes ( )No	( )Yes ( )No	( )Yes ( )No
Total Scheduled Walking Time (Or Other Aerobic Workout)	Aerobic Workout **REST DAY**	Aerobic Workout 	Aerobic Workout **45 min.**
Working Heart Rate	_____% = _____bpm	_____% = _____bpm	70 % = _____bpm
Body Parts (Listed By Priority)	Body Part Workout 1._____ × _____ sets 2._____ × _____ sets 3._____ × _____ sets 4._____ × _____ sets 5._____ × _____ sets	Body Part Workout 1._____ × 3 sets 2._____ × 2 sets 3._____ × 2 sets 4._____ × 1 sets 5._____ × 1 sets	Body Part Workout 1._____ × 2 sets 2._____ × 1 sets 3._____ × 1 sets 4._____ × 1 sets 5._____ × 0 sets
Cool-Down Exercises	( )Yes ( )No	( )Yes ( )No	( )Yes ( )No
Notes/Comments On Today's Workout			

WEDNESDAY	THURSDAY	FRIDAY	SATURDAY
_____ bpm	_____ bpm	_____ bpm	_____ bpm
( )Yes ( )No	( )Yes ( )No	( )Yes ( )No	( )Yes ( )No
Aerobic Workout	Aerobic Workout	Aerobic Workout	Aerobic Workout
25 min.	**30 min.**		**60 min.**
_60_ % = _____ bpm	_70_ % = _____ bpm	____ % = _____ bpm	_70_ % = _____ bpm
Body Part Workout	Body Part Workout	Body Part Workout	Body Part Workout
1._____ × _____ sets 2._____ × _____ sets 3._____ × _____ sets 4._____ × _____ sets 5._____ × _____ sets	1._____ × 2 sets 2._____ × 2 sets 3._____ × 2 sets 4._____ × 1 sets 5._____ × 1 sets	1._____ × 1 sets 2._____ × 2 sets 3._____ × 3 sets 4._____ × 2 sets 5._____ × 1 sets	1._____ × 3 sets 2._____ × 3 sets 3._____ × 2 sets 4._____ × 2 sets 5._____ × 1 sets
( )Yes ( )No	( )Yes ( )No	( )Yes ( )No	( )Yes ( )No

WEEK 26

My Working Pulse Rate	SUNDAY	MONDAY	TUESDAY
60% = _____ bpm 70% = _____ bpm 80% = _____ bpm			
Resting Pulse Rate	_____ bpm	_____ bpm	_____ bpm
Warm-Up Exercises	( )Yes ( )No	( )Yes ( )No	( )Yes ( )No
Total Scheduled Walking Time (Or Other Aerobic Workout)	Aerobic Workout **REST DAY**	Aerobic Workout	Aerobic Workout **45 min.**
Working Heart Rate	_____ % = _____ bpm	_____ % = _____ bpm	60 % = _____ bpm
Body Parts (Listed By Priority)	Body Part Workout 1._____ × _____ sets 2._____ × _____ sets 3._____ × _____ sets 4._____ × _____ sets 5._____ × _____ sets	Body Part Workout 1._____ × 3 sets 2._____ × 3 sets 3._____ × 2 sets 4._____ × 2 sets 5._____ × 1 sets	Body Part Workout 1._____ × 2 sets 2._____ × 2 sets 3._____ × 1 sets 4._____ × 1 sets 5._____ × 1 sets
Cool-Down Exercises	( )Yes ( )No	( )Yes ( )No	( )Yes ( )No
Notes/Comments On Today's Workout			

A Half Year In Your Life . . .

WEDNESDAY	THURSDAY	FRIDAY	SATURDAY
_____ bpm	_____ bpm	_____ bpm	_____ bpm
( )Yes ( )No	( )Yes ( )No	( )Yes ( )No	( )Yes ( )No
Aerobic Workout	Aerobic Workout	Aerobic Workout	Aerobic Workout
30 min.	30 min.		60 min.
60 % = _____ bpm	70 % = _____ bpm	_____ % = _____ bpm	70 % = _____ bpm
Body Part Workout	Body Part Workout	Body Part Workout	Body Part Workout
1._____ × _____ sets 2._____ × _____ sets 3._____ × _____ sets 4._____ × _____ sets 5._____ × _____ sets	1._____ × 2 sets 2._____ × 2 sets 3._____ × 2 sets 4._____ × 1 sets 5._____ × 1 sets	1._____ × 1 sets 2._____ × 2 sets 3._____ × 3 sets 4._____ × 2 sets 5._____ × 1 sets	1._____ × 3 sets 2._____ × 3 sets 3._____ × 2 sets 4._____ × 2 sets 5._____ × 1 sets
( )Yes ( )No	( )Yes ( )No	( )Yes ( )No	( )Yes ( )No

Chapter 9

A Total Body Program For Life

Now that you have completed six months of my program of aerobic fitness, body specific exercises, and general fitness, it is time to evaluate your response to it.

Your response should be based upon several factors:

1. Your ability to consistently do the workouts called for without unusual weariness or soreness.

2. Your body's general response to the workouts: Did you feel energized? Did you sleep more soundly? Did you feel rested? Did you achieve a higher state of overall fitness?

3. Your body's specific response to the workouts: Did your problem body areas begin to improve? Did they improve to the point that you re-evaluated them periodically and made adjustments to move other problems areas into top priority spots when your top priority body parts improved?

Let's work backwards on those areas.

Ideally, you should have seen some improvements in the body parts you first picked as needing work. If you kept the priorities you began with, the improvements should have been pronounced. If you periodically re-evaluated your priorities, you should have experienced a more well-rounded toning up of your body: by that I mean that you should have experienced a general improvement in muscle tone and in body image. (Keep in mind that body parts that have shown improvement are likely to need maintenance, so attempt to keep your original top priority body part on the program at all times, even if only at number five priority.) Additionally, the general program should have gradually built muscle, burned fat, and generally brought an improvement on all fronts—especially in your self-image.

This moves us into the second factor, the general increase in fitness (and health) a regular program bestows. Your doctor should have seen improvements on his charting of your general health. Your resting pulse rate should have lowered a bit more, your blood pressure may have gone down a bit, your body weight may have dropped somewhat (or it may not have, if you built a great deal of muscle tissue while losing fat, since muscle weighs more than fat), your body dimensions may have become more customized.

Objectively speaking, how do you look physically as opposed to six months ago?

Your energy levels should be higher, your sleep patterns more regular and rest-restorative, your alertness should have picked up from increased blood flow, you should be enjoying bowel regularity, and you may have even noticed a shift in your dietary habits with a tendency to crave more carbohydrates and less meat protein.

Do you generally feel more alive?

Were you able to handle the workouts without too much stress and strain?

Hopefully, based upon our discussions of the week- and month-long trial periods, if the workouts became too much for you, you backed off, gradually worked yourself to a higher level of fitness, and then restarted the program.

If the program was challenging but not intimidating, you've obviously adapted to the early parts of the book and have followed the program logically and well.

If the program was helpful but inadequate for your needs, we have a solution for that, also.

CUSTOMIZING THE PROGRAM FOR THE REST OF YOUR LIFE

There are, then, three alternatives that faced you during or near the end of the six-month program: either it was too difficult, it was right on, or it was not difficult enough. There are three ways to customize the program for the year coming up. (Please keep in mind that these customizations need not be based merely upon your response to the six months just past, but are workable in the event you want to plan the upcoming six months as a more challenging period or a less challenging period in your ongoing fitness lifestyle.)

I want the coming six months to be easier than the last six.

1. In the Total Scheduled Walking Time boxes, subtract 5 minutes from every time indicated that is less than 60 minutes; subtract 10 minutes from every time indicated that is 60 minutes or more.

2. Keep the Working Heart Rates the same as the six months past.

3. Under the Body Parts, subtract 1 set from each and every one of the body parts you've listed; if that makes some of the body parts come out with a 0, that's fine—just don't work on those body parts that day.

4. Don't work out at all on Wednesdays. Turn Wednesdays into a second Rest Day.

I loved the six months' workout.

1. This is the easiest of all. Merely recopy the six months onto a set of blank pages, and begin again at Week 1.

I enjoyed the six months just past, but I now need more challenge.

1. In the Total Scheduled Walking Time boxes, add 5 minutes to every time indicated that is less than 60 minutes; add 10 minutes to every time indicated that is 60 minutes or more.

2. Keep the Working Heart Rate the same as the six months past.

3. Under the Body Parts, add 1 more set to the priority (the number 1) body part listed for each workout; add 1 set to the second priority body part on odd numbered weeks, and add 1 set to the third priority body part on even numbered weeks.

It is that easy. Now you've got an easier six months ahead of you, the same six months ahead of you (with the ongoing option to at any time re-evaluate the priority list of body parts and to make adjustments), or a more challenging six months ahead of you.

At the end of each half year, repeat this evaluation, and make whatever adjustments you feel necessary for your fitness level and fitness goals.

The program is extremely flexible when adjusted using the above guidelines. You can make your own adjustments for the rest of your life. Be fit. Be happy. Live long. Live well.